150
Things to Make
and Do with Peppa

Ladybird Books is part of the Penguin Random House group of companies
whose addresses can be found at global.penguinrandomhouse.com.
Published by Penguin Random House Children's: 80 Strand, London WC2R 0RL, UK
Penguin Random House Australia Pty Ltd: 707 Collins Street, Melbourne, VIC 3008
Penguin Random House New Zealand: 67 Apollo Drive, Rosedale, Auckland 0632
www.penguin.co.uk   www.puffin.co.uk   www.ladybird.co.uk

Penguin
Random House
UK

First published 2017
001

Adapted by Sue Nicholson
Step-by-step illustrations by Helen Hurry
Photography by Neil Hall. Photography for Makes 95 and 96 by Nina Tara.
With thanks to Evelyn Hall, Darshan Iyngkaran, Priya Mistry, Alana Powell,
Shakiel Qayyum, Bertie Ray and Boaz Reuben

This book is based on the TV series *Peppa Pig*.
Peppa Pig is created by Neville Astley and Mark Baker.
Peppa Pig © Astley Baker Davies Ltd/Entertainment One UK Ltd 2003.
www.peppapig.com

Printed in Slovakia
A CIP catalogue record for this book is available from the British Library
ISBN: 978-0-241-29398-0

All correspondence to:
Ladybird Books
Penguin Random House Children's
80 Strand, London WC2R 0RL

Peppa Pig

150
Things to Make
and Do with Peppa

How to Use this Book

The activities in this book have been devised and written for big piggies to do with their little piggies and include plenty of ideas for games to play and for fun days out, as well as for things to make and bake.

All of the activities require some level of supervision, depending on the age and ability of your little piggy. For example, while older children will be able to manage some of the craft activities with minimal supervision, younger children will need close supervision at all times and many of the steps should be done for them. No matter what the age and ability of your child, **always** do yourself any steps that involve the use of an oven, scissors or knives.

Although all the activities in this book require adult help, those that need particularly close supervision have been given the following icon:

Templates

Templates are included for some of the craft activities. Either photocopy the templates directly on to A4 card, or trace on to tracing paper (or baking parchment) and glue on to card before cutting them out.

Craft Activity Tips and Techniques

* Let your little piggy help decide which activity to do, so you can talk about what you need and the best time (and place) to do it.

* Make sure you have everything you need and enough time to complete each activity before you begin.

* Start a collection of craft materials, such as scraps of fabric or tissue paper, old buttons, and recycled boxes, bottles and cardboard tubes.

* Invest in some strong, good-quality PVA glue. As well as being good for sticking, it makes a good 'varnish' when mixed with water – paint a coat on a finished, dry papier-mâché or salt-dough model so it looks shiny and lasts longer. (The glue will look milky at first but dries to a clear, hard finish.)

* Protect any work surfaces and make sure your little piggy is wearing an apron or an old T-shirt so they can have lots of messy fun.

* Do any steps that require adult help but try to let your child do as much of each activity as possible, such as painting or sticking. Try not to take over too much!

* Don't forget to give plenty of praise and encouragement – including getting your little piggy to help clean up afterwards!

Story Time

If you want a quiet, non-messy activity, try one of the story-starter activities to spark your child's creative imagination, such as *Once Upon a Time . . .* (number 42) or *Make Up a Space Story* (number 112).

Peppa and George love this book. We hope you do, too! Snort! Snort!

Contents

1 Peppa's House

Build a house like Peppa's, with a red tiled roof and yellow walls.

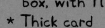

You will need:
* Square cardboard box, with flaps
* Thick card
* Masking tape
* Pencil
* Scissors
* Thin white, blue and red card
* PVA glue
* Paintbrush
* Poster or acrylic paints
* Black pipe cleaners or cocktail sticks

1

Cut four pieces of thick card, the same size and shape as the box's flaps.

2

Stick the card to the flaps. Tape the two longer flaps together to make the roof.

3

Hold the smaller flaps up and draw along the shape of the roof on each flap.

4

Fold along the pencil lines towards the roof and push the corners inside.

5

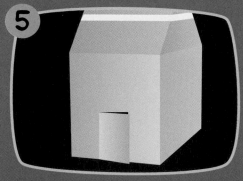

Cut out a front door, leaving one side attached, so the door can open and close.

6

Paint the house the same colours as Peppa's house, then glue on the windows.

7

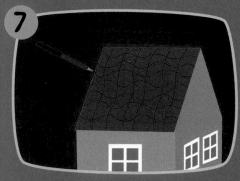

Glue sheets of red card to the sloped roof. Use red paint or a red pen to draw on the tiles.

8

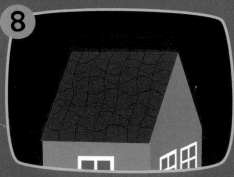

Make an aerial out of black pipe cleaners or black-painted cocktail sticks.

To make the windows:

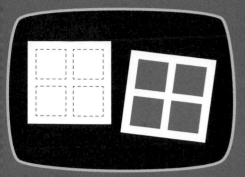

Cut out squares of white card as shown. Cut out four squares in each to make the window frames. Glue a piece of blue card behind each window, then stick them to the side of the house.

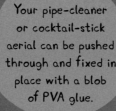

Your pipe-cleaner or cocktail-stick aerial can be pushed through and fixed in place with a blob of PVA glue.

2 Peppa and George

Make a mini Peppa and mini George to play in your house!

You will need:
* Card
* Scissors
* Paints or coloured pencils
* Craft sticks
* PVA glue

templates

Copy or trace the templates on to card. Cut them out, colour them in, then glue them on to craft sticks. Snort!

3 Peppa's Car

Beep! Beep! It's Peppa's little red car. Where are Peppa and her family going today?

You will need:
* Card
* Scissors
* Paints or coloured pencils
* Craft stick
* PVA glue

Copy or trace the template on to card. Cut it out, colour in, then glue on to a craft stick. Brrrm!

Beep! Beep!

Peppa's Ears

Use the templates to make some pink Peppa ears. Snort! Hee Hee!

You will need:
* Thin dark pink card and light pink card
* Scissors
* PVA glue
* Pencil

1 Copy or trace the large ear templates on to thin dark pink card, then cut them out.

2 Cut two strips of card, 5cm x 30cm. Glue them together to make one long headband.

3 Measure the headband to fit round your little piggy's head, then glue or tape the ends together.

4 Copy or trace the smaller inner ear templates on to thin light pink card, then cut them out. Stick them on to the main ear pieces.

5 Glue the two Peppa ears on to the middle of the headband. Snort!

Inner ear template – light pink card

Main ear template – dark pink card

Inner ear template – light pink card

Main ear template – dark pink card

Oink!

Hee! Hee!

Oink!

5 Grampy Rabbit's Submarine

Ahoy there! Grampy Rabbit's submarine is made out of bits of rubbish. You can make this one out of papier mâché!

You will need:
* Sausage-shaped balloon
* Old newspaper
* PVA glue
* Water
* Large bowl
* Yoghurt pot
* Bendy straw
* Scissors
* Toothpick
* Plastic bottle
* Black and white paint
* Paintbrush
* Black card
* Safety pin
* Masking tape

To make papier mâché:
- Mix together one part PVA glue and three parts water in a large bowl.
- Tear sheets of old newspaper into long thin strips, around 2cm wide x 5cm long.
- Soak the strips in the glue mix. Overlap the strips as you paste them on to your balloon.

1

Blow up a sausage-shaped balloon and cover it in 5–6 layers of papier mâché. When it is dry, pop the balloon with a safety pin.

2

Ask an adult to make a hole with scissors in the base of a yoghurt pot and push the top of a bendy straw through the hole.

3

Use masking tape to stick the pot to the top of your balloon. Cover the pot and straw in 2–3 layers of papier mâché.

4

When all the papier mâché is dry, mix together black and white paint to make different shades of grey.

5

Paint a patchwork design all over the submarine. Print rivets with the end of a paintbrush.

6

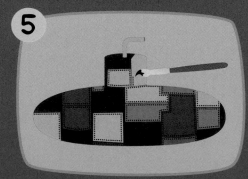

Cut a propeller from the side of a plastic bottle and stick it to the end of a toothpick.

propeller cut from the side of a plastic bottle.

toothpick

7

Glue on a porthole cut from black card, and push in the toothpick propeller at one end.

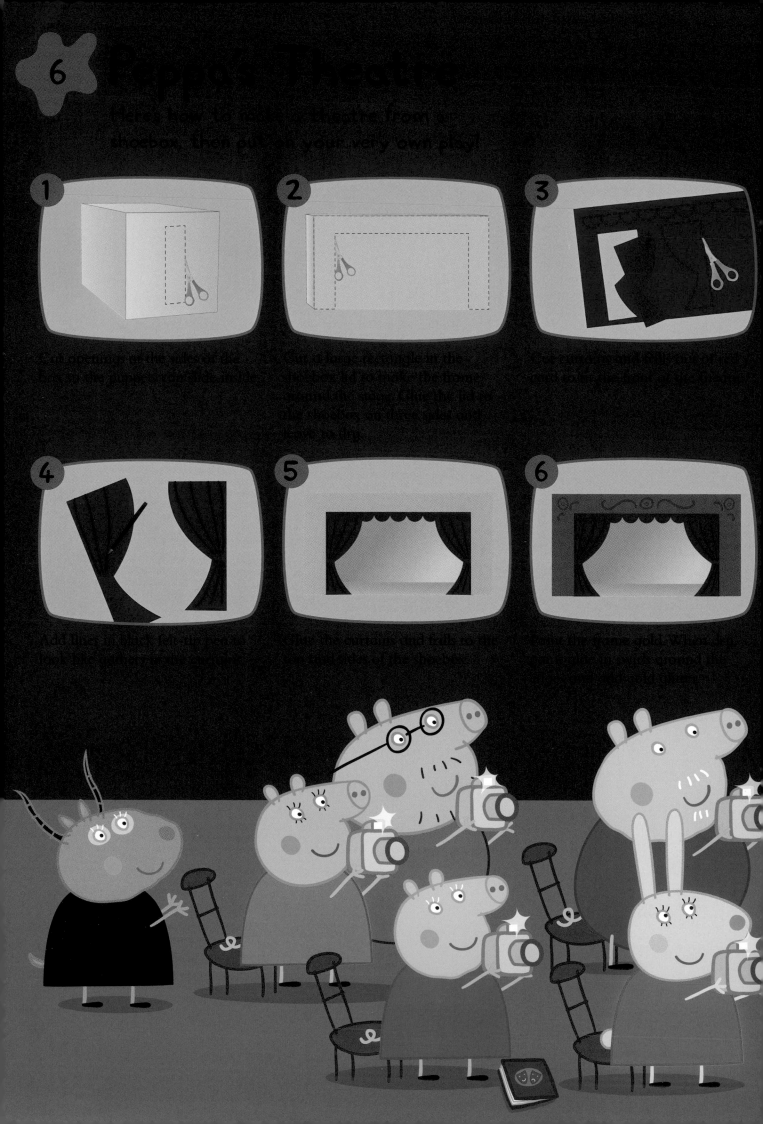

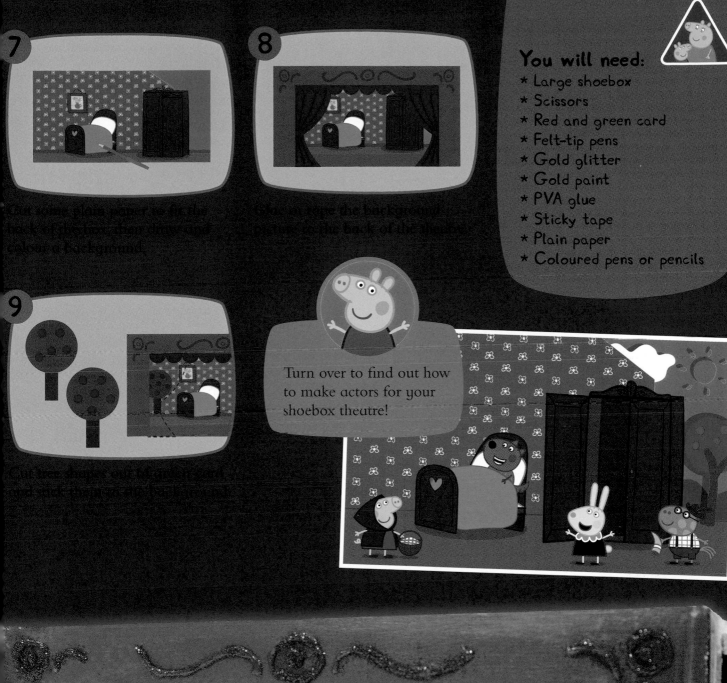

7 Cut some plain paper to fit the back of the box, then draw and colour a background.

8 Use to tape the background picture to the back of the box.

9 Cut tree shapes out of green card and stick them to the box picture.

Turn over to find out how to make actors for your shoebox theatre!

You will need:
* Large shoebox
* Scissors
* Red and green card
* Felt-tip pens
* Gold glitter
* Gold paint
* PVA glue
* Sticky tape
* Plain paper
* Coloured pens or pencils

7 Put on a Play

Make puppets and put on Peppa's school play in your shoebox theatre.

You will need:
* Shoebox theatre
* Cardboard
* Scissors
* Coloured pens or pencils
* Craft sticks
* PVA glue

1 Copy or trace the templates below on to cardboard and cut them out.

2 Colour the cardboard characters to match the ones in the pictures opposite.

3 Glue each of the puppets to the end of a long craft stick.

8 Fairy Wings

These pretty fairy wings are made from layers of tissue paper sprinkled with glitter and stars.

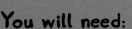

You will need:
* Cellophane
* 8-10 sheets tissue paper
* Diluted PVA glue (1 part glue, 3 parts water)
* Paintbrush
* Glitter
* Tiny hearts and stars
* Scissors
* Thick card
* Hole punch
* Two 40cm lengths of elastic
* Sheet of A4 paper

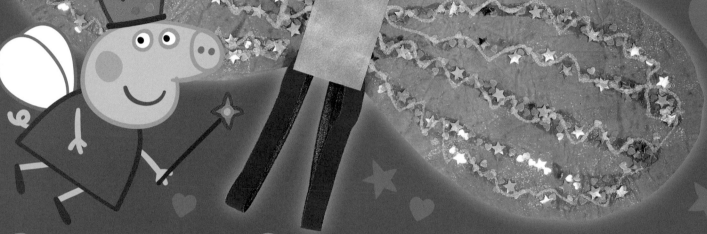

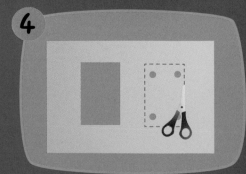

1 Lay a sheet of tissue paper over a piece of cellophane.

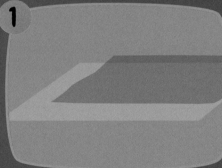

2 Brush the PVA mixture over the paper. Lay another sheet of tissue on top.

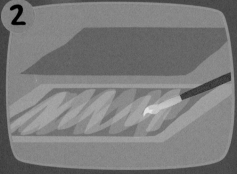

3 Add the rest of the tissue paper, in layers, brushing the PVA mixture between each layer.

4 Cut two pieces of thick card 5cm x 8cm. Make holes in each long side of one of the pieces with a hole punch, as shown.

5 Thread one piece of elastic through the top and bottom holes on the left side.

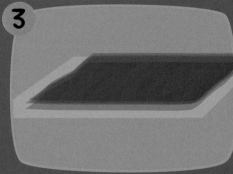

6 Knot the ends together, then do the same on the right with the other piece of elastic.

7

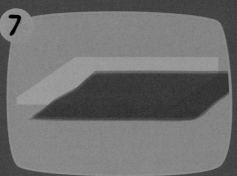

When it's dry, peel the hardened tissue paper off the cellophane.

8

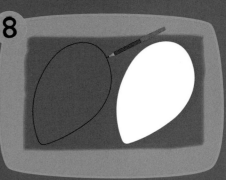

Draw a teardrop shape on a sheet of A4 paper and cut it out. Use this as a template for tracing around on the tissue paper and then cut out two shapes for the wings.

9

Glue the wings on to the card in the centre, overlapping the pointed ends in the middle. Glue the second piece of card in the middle on the other side to hide the ends of the wings under the card.

10

Brush glue on the top of the wings and the card, then sprinkle with glitter and tiny hearts and stars.

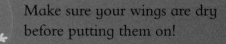

Make sure your wings are dry before putting them on!

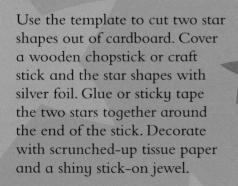

9 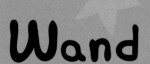 # Wand

Swish! Swish! Make a wish with this pretty fairy wand.

Use the template to cut two star shapes out of cardboard. Cover a wooden chopstick or craft stick and the star shapes with silver foil. Glue or sticky tape the two stars together around the end of the stick. Decorate with scrunched-up tissue paper and a shiny stick-on jewel.

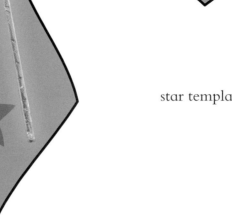

star template

Frilly Fairy Skirt

Peppa loves parties! This year she's going to have a fancy-dress birthday party and dress up as a fairy princess. Here's how to make a fairy-princess costume so you can look just like Peppa!

You will need:
* White or pink ribbon or elastic
* Coloured netting
* Scissors
* Needle and thread (if using elastic)

1 Ask a grown-up to cut the elastic or ribbon to fit round your waist, plus an extra 25cm–30cm for the bow if using ribbon.

2 Measure the netting into strips of fabric twice the length of your skirt. E.g. if you'd like your skirt to be 30cm long, your strips need to be 60cm long.

3 Cut 20 strips. The thicker you cut the strips, the fluffier your skirt will be!

4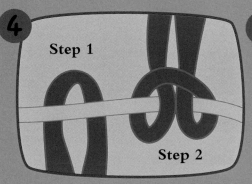

Step 1

Step 2

Fold your strip in half to create a loop at the top. Place the strip under the ribbon or elastic, so that the loop sticks out at the top, and pull the ends through the loop. Pull the knot tight.

5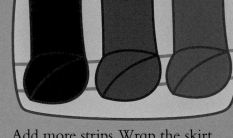

Add more strips. Wrap the skirt around your waist and tie the ribbon in a bow. If you have used elastic, ask a grown-up to sew the ends together.

Fairy Princess Tiara

Use the template to make a glittery tiara fit for a fairy princess.

You will need:
* Glitter card
* Scissors
* PVA glue or sticky tape
* Decorations, such as stick-on gems or foam shapes
* Paperclips

1. Trace the tiara template on to the back of the glitter card, then cut it out.

2. Cut a long strip of card with a width of 4cm to make the headband.

3. Glue or tape one end of the tiara and headband together.

4. Decorate with foam shapes and stick-on gems.

5. Measure the headband to fit round your little piggy's head, then glue or tape the ends together.

Hold the pieces in place with paperclips, while the glue dries.

stick-on gems

tiara template

12 Tooth Fairy Envelope

Pop a baby tooth in this little envelope and see if the tooth fairy swaps it for a shiny coin!

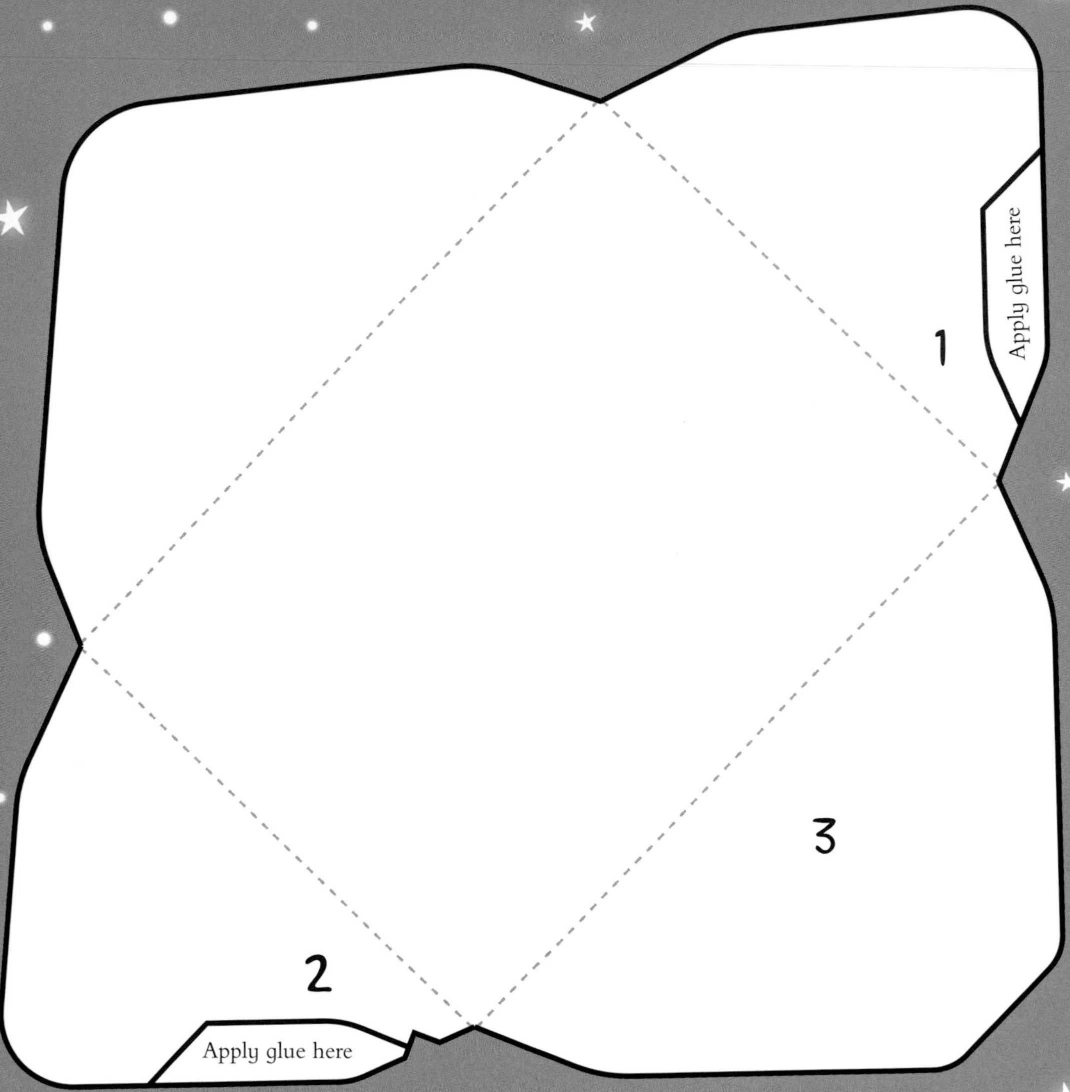

Apply glue here

1

3

2

Apply glue here

You will need:
* Paper
* PVA glue
* Felt-tip pens
* Scissors

1 Trace or photocopy the template.

2 Fold flaps 1 and 2 away from you.

3 Turn envelope over and apply glue to tabs.

4 Fold flap 3 inwards and stick it to the tabs. Decorate your envelope with pens.

5 Fold the final flap inwards and pop your tooth inside before tucking the flap in, ready for the tooth fairy.

13 Pretty Fabric Bag

Turn an old, plain fabric tote into this pretty bag, decorated with Peppa pink hearts and flowers!

You will need:
* Ironed canvas tote bag
* Card
* Plain fabric
* Fabric glue
* Embroidery thread
* Needle
* Buttons
* Coloured felt
* Pinking shears or scissors

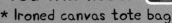

1 Trace or copy the templates below on to card and use them to cut the shapes out of fabric or felt. For fabric, use pinking shears so the edges do not fray. For felt, you can decorate the edges with a blanket stitch.

2 Arrange the hearts and flowers on the front of the bag and glue them in position with fabric glue.

template

Sew on small buttons for the flower centres.

How to do blanket stitch:

1 Knot the end of the thread and push the needle down through the fabric about 5mm away from the edge and pull through.

2 Push the needle down through the fabric again just to the right of your first stitch. Pull the needle through the loop.

3 Push the needle down again through the fabric about 5mm to the right of your last hole and pull through the loop. Repeat this last step until you have stitched all the way round.

14 Fairy-tale Castle

Here's how to make your very own fairy-tale castle!

You will need:
* 1 large cardboard box
* 4 smaller cardboard boxes (long)
* Scissors
* PVA glue
* Pencil
* Thin red and blue card
* Cocktail sticks
* Paints
* Paintbrush
* Silver and gold metallic pens

Who's going to live in your fairy-tale castle?

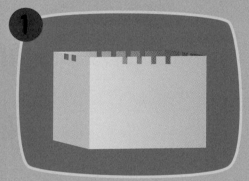

1 Cut the flaps off the top of the large box, then cut squares in the top to look like battlements.

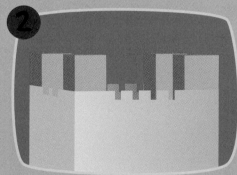

2 Glue one of the long, small boxes into each corner of the bigger box.

3 Cut battlements in the top of each tower. Draw an arched doorway on the front of the castle.

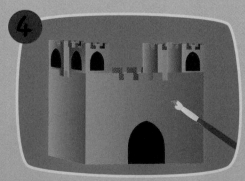

4 Paint the castle yellow. When dry, paint the entrance brown and add some black arched windows.

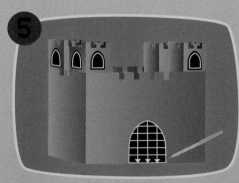

5 Use a silver metallic pen to draw crisscross lines over the brown doorway to make a portcullis.

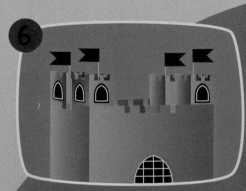

6 Make flags out of red card glued on to cocktail sticks and add one to the top of each tower.

15 ✳ Fairy Cakes

These princess fairy cakes are delicious! Decorate them with cherries and pink icing. Yum!

You will need:
* 100g unsalted butter (softened)
* 100g caster sugar
* 2 eggs, beaten
* 100g self-raising flour
* ½ teaspoon baking powder
* 12 paper cases
* Baking tray

To decorate:
* 200g icing sugar
* Milk or water, as required
* Food colouring (optional)
* 6 glacé cherries, halved

1 Heat the oven to 200°C (gas mark 6) and fill a baking tray with 12 paper cases.

2 Beat together the sugar and butter (with a spoon or electric mixer) until the mixture turns pale and creamy.

3 Add the beaten eggs a little at a time.

4 Fold in the flour and baking powder.

5 Divide the mixture into the paper cases.

6 Bake for 15–20 minutes until golden brown, then leave to cool.

Make up the icing sugar according to the instructions on the packet. If you like, add a drop of pink food colouring. Put half a glacé cherry on top of each cake.

16 Time for Tea

Have a princess tea party for your friends. Serve princess fairy cakes on dainty plates and ask your friends to come dressed in their very best princess costumes.

17 The Princess and the Frog

Look! Her Royal Highness Princess Peppa is having a party at the palace. All the fairy princesses are having a lovely time when suddenly a green frog hops out of the fountain.

"If you kiss a frog, it may turn into a handsome prince," says Princess Suzy Sheep.

"Yuck, I'm not ever kissing a frog!" says Princess Peppa.

Make up the rest of the story to see what happens next.

Valentine Cards

Make one of these cards for someone special on Valentine's Day!

You will need:
* Folded coloured card
* Tissue paper
* Wrapping paper
* PVA glue
* Scissors
* Stick-on gems

Draw the outline of a large heart on the front of the card and glue on lots of tiny balls of scrunched-up tissue paper.

Cut heart shapes out of wrapping paper and glue them on to the front of a card on top of each other or in a row. Decorate with stick-on gems around the edges.

Valentine Heart

You will need:
* Card
* Pencil
* Felt
* Ribbon
* Cotton wool
* Embroidery thread
* Needle
* Fabric glue
* Scissors

1

2

3

4

hanging ribbon

Decorate the edge of the heart with blanket stitch.

heart templates

See Make 13 for how to sew blanket stitch.

20 Friendship Bracelets

Peppa and Suzy Sheep are busy making friendship bracelets. Here's how you can make some, too.

You will need:
* Embroidery thread
* Sticky tape
* Scissors
* Beads

1

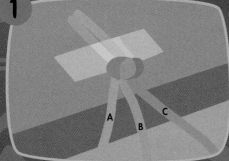

Choose three lengths of different-coloured thread. Knot the three ends together, then tape the knot to a tabletop.

2

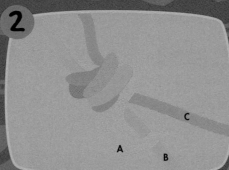

Hold thread B with your left hand. Loop thread A round B, then thread the end through the loop to make a knot.

3

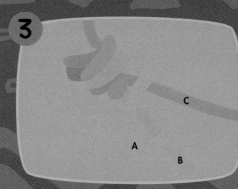

Pull the knot tight, then repeat, to make a second knot, so you have two knots on thread B.

4

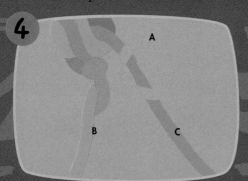

Hold thread C with your left hand. Loop thread A round C, then thread the end through the loop to make a knot.

5

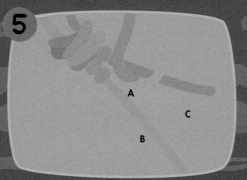

Pull the knot tight, then repeat, to make a second knot, so you have two knots on thread C.

6

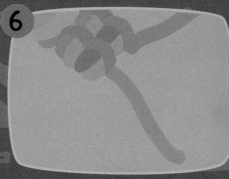

Start the next row, making knots from left to right, following the pattern in the panel at the top of the opposite page.

7

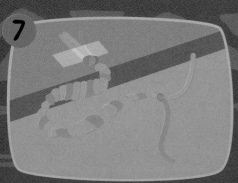

Keep knotting the threads until you have made a bracelet that is long enough to fit round your friend's wrist.

8

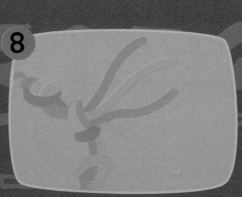

Trim the ends of the thread, making sure they are long enough to tie on the bracelet.

Thread some beads on to your bracelet as you make the knots.

Row 1:

Knot A twice on to B.
Knot A twice on to C.

Row 2:

Knot B twice on to C.
Knot B twice on to A.

Row 3:

Knot C twice on to A.
Knot C twice on to B.

21 Mummy Pig's Day Daffodil

Peppa is making Mummy Pig a pretty daffodil in a pot to say "Happy Mummy Pig's Day!"

You will need:
* Yellow and green cardboard
* Pencil
* Scissors
* Eggbox
* Coloured tissue paper
* PVA glue
* Short green garden cane or green straw
* Ribbons
* Modelling clay
* Plant pot
* Paints
* Paintbrush

1 Copy or trace the daffodil flower templates on to bright yellow cardboard. Cut out the flowers.

2 Tear a cup shape from an eggbox, paint it dark yellow or orange, and glue to main flower shape when dry.

3 Glue some scrunched-up tissue paper inside the eggbox compartment.

4 Tape the flower to the end of a green garden cane or straw.

5 Draw some long daffodil leaves on to green card, cut them out and glue on to the stick.

6 Push the bottom of the stick into a lump of modelling clay and wedge it in a pretty pot.

daffodil flower template

daffodil flower template

Add scrunched-up tissue paper for soil in your pot and tie pretty ribbons around it to decorate!

This daffodil makes a lovely Mother's Day present for your Mummy Pig!

22 Spring Flowers

Look out for the first flowers of the year in your garden or the park. Can you spot any tiny white snowdrops or bright yellow daffodils?

23 Tulip Prints

Print a row of tulips to make a picture for your wall, a pretty birthday card or some wrapping paper!

You will need:
* Potatoes
* Knife
* Acrylic or poster paints
* Saucers
* Thin cardboard
* Thick cardboard
* Hole punch

1. Cut a potato in half, then cut away the flesh to leave a tulip shape.

2. Dip the potato into saucers of paint and print a row of colourful tulips on to thin cardboard.

3. Print the green stems by dipping the edge of a piece of thick cardboard into green paint.

4. Print the leaves with the tips of your fingers – one print for each leaf!

hole made with hole punch

Printed tulips make pretty cards and gift tags!

Emily Elephant's White Mouse

Squeak! Squeak! This little white mouse is just like Emily Elephant's.

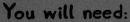

You will need:
* Salt dough (recipe below)
* Rolling pin
* String
* Scissors
* Water
* Paintbrush
* Acrylic paint
* PVA glue

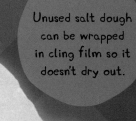

Unused salt dough can be wrapped in cling film so it doesn't dry out.

1

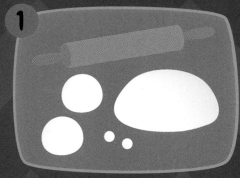

Roll and shape some salt dough into a mouse shape.

2

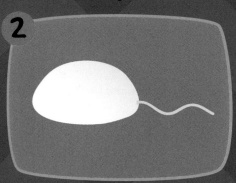

Cut a piece of string to make a tail. Make a slit in the bottom of the mouse's body and push the end of the string into it, covering with dough to seal.

Squeak!

To make salt dough:
- Mix together 100g salt and 240g plain flour in a mixing bowl.
- Slowly add 250–350ml of lukewarm water and mix into a dough.
- Knead the dough for around 3–5 minutes until it is smooth.
- Bake models in the bottom of an oven (at 150°C, gas mark 2) for around three hours, then leave to cool.

3

Shape the ears and eyes out of dough and attach to the mouse's body with a little water. Use the end of a paintbrush to give the mouse a smile!

4 Bake, leave to cool, paint with acrylic paint and then varnish with PVA glue when dry. (See Make 46 for instructions.)

Chinese Lanterns

Make some pretty paper lanterns
to hang up at Chinese New Year!

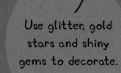

Use glitter, gold
stars and shiny
gems to decorate.

Cut a strip off the end of a sheet
of A4 paper to make the handle.

Fold the paper in half lengthways,
then make cuts across the fold.
Leave 2cm–3cm at the edge.

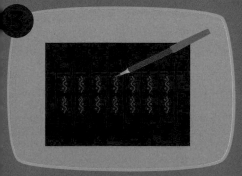

Draw a pattern on the lantern
with a metallic pen, glue on strips
of patterned paper or add shiny
stickers or gems.

Glue the edges together to make
the lantern shape, then glue the
handle so the ends are inside the
top of the lantern.

Pretty Easter Eggs

Here's how to make an eggbox full of pretty decorated Easter eggs!

You will need:
* 6 eggs
* Eggbox
* PVA glue
* Paintbrush
* Coloured tissue paper
* Paints
* Thin card
* Ribbon
* Scissors

1 Crack an egg in half, pour out the insides and wash it carefully. Glue the shell back together along the edges.

2 Cover the whole egg in glue, then add 3–4 layers of torn-up scraps of tissue paper.

3 When dry, paint a pretty pattern on the egg with paint.

4 Photocopy the pictures below and stick them on to some card. Carefully cut them out and attach each one to some ribbon around the centre of each egg.

5 Decorate your eggbox with scraps of tissue, or paint it.

To blow an egg:
If you prefer, you can ask an adult to blow the yolk and white out of each egg before you decorate it. Prick a tiny hole in the top and bottom of each egg with a darning needle. Hold the egg over a bowl and blow gently through the top hole, until all the egg white and yolk have dripped out of the bottom.

Easter Bunnies

Make some cute bouncy bunnies out of card tubes.

You will need:
* Cardboard tubes
* Paint
* Paintbrush
* Card
* PVA glue
* Googly eyes
* Felt-tip pen
* Cotton wool
* Scissors

Cut out and stick different coloured card to the inside of the ears.

googly eyes

white card teeth

cotton-wool tail

rabbit ears and feet template

1 Paint a cardboard tube any colour you like.

2 Copy or trace the template on to card to make two long rabbit ears and two big feet, and cut them out. Paint the ears and feet to match the bunny's body, then glue them on to the top and bottom of the tube.

3 Stick on two googly eyes. Cut a triangle out of pink card for the nose and a white rectangle for the teeth. Draw on a mouth and whiskers with a felt-tip pen. Don't forget to give your bunny a cotton-wool tail!

28 Easter Bonnet

Peppa loves her Easter bonnet! Create your own beautiful bonnet by following these simple steps!

You will need:
* Old straw hat
* Scissors
* Coloured card
* Coloured foam
* Coloured tissue paper
* Glue
* 3 polystyrene eggs
* 80cm of yellow ribbon

1

Cut the ribbon in half and stick or sew one piece to each side of the inside rim of the hat, to make the ribbon ties.

2

Cover each polystyrene egg in glue, then add 2–3 layers of torn-up scraps of tissue paper.

3

To make the flowers, trace the templates on to coloured card and cut out the shapes.

4

Use your fingers to gently press each petal in one by one. This will give each flower a realistic shape and realistic dimensions.

5

Layer and glue your coloured flower pieces together, using the different sizes and circles to form the centres.

6

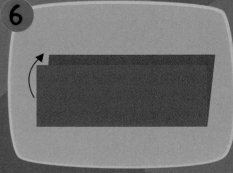

To make the feathers, cut the foam to 15cm x 21cm in size. Then fold in half lengthways to make a long rectangle.

7

Cut the rectangle of foam into a semicircle shape and then cut triangles out along the curved edge. Open the shape out. Make two more feathers in different colours.

8

Once all of the pieces are dry, arrange them on the hat and glue them in place.

29 Easter Basket

Make this little Easter basket to hold some tiny chocolate eggs.

You will need:
* ★ Wrapping paper
* ★ Pencil
* ★ Ruler
* ★ Scissors
* ★ PVA glue
* ★ Coloured straw or shredded paper
* ★ Chocolate eggs
* ★ Coloured card

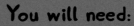

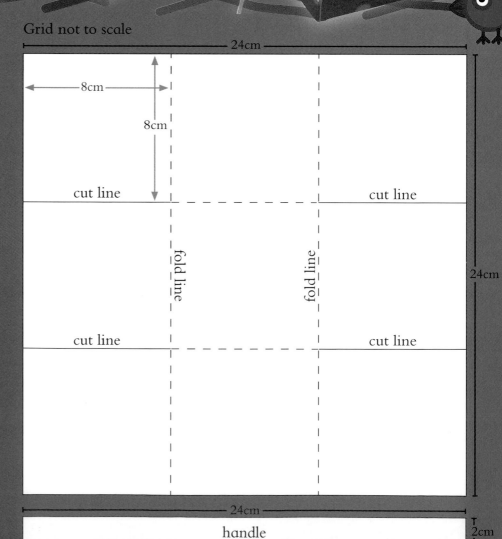

1 Measure and draw the grid 24cm x 24cm on to a piece of coloured card.

2 Stick a sheet of wrapping paper on the other side – this will be the outside of the basket.

3 Cut the four lines, as marked, from the edges to the central square.

4 Fold the card to the centre.

5 Overlap and glue together at the sides.

6 Cut out a handle of more wrapping-paper-lined card and glue inside the basket.

7 Fill the basket with coloured straw or shredded paper. Now you can pop in some tiny chocolate eggs – yummy!

Grid not to scale

24cm

8cm

8cm

8cm

cut line   cut line

fold line   fold line

cut line   cut line

24cm

24cm

24cm

handle

2cm

30 Easter Egg Hunt

Have fun like Peppa and George, looking for Easter eggs that Mummy and Daddy Pig have hidden in the garden!

31 Egg Necklace

Peppa has hidden a toy inside her egg-shaped necklace. What are you going to hide in yours?

You will need:
* 2 eggs
* Newspaper
* PVA glue/water
* Scissors
* Paints
* Paintbrush
* Wool or embroidery thread

See Make 5 for how to make papier mâché.

1

Hard boil two eggs, cool, then cover ¾ of each egg in 4–5 layers of papier mâché. Leave to dry.

2

Remove the top of each egg. Scoop out the insides and shells, then cut a zigzag edge on each paper egg.

3

Paint the outside and the inside of the eggs. Make two holes next to each other in the top and bottom of each egg.

4

Make a long friendship bracelet (see Make 20), or plait three strands of wool into a chain.

5

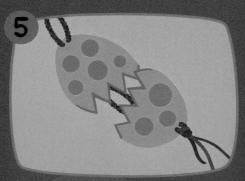

Thread both ends of the chain through the top of one egg and out of the bottom of the other. Knot the wool below the bottom egg and leave the ends loose.

Now your necklace is ready to wear!

Rebecca Rabbit's Ears

Use the templates to make some Rebecca Rabbit ears.

1 Copy or trace the large ear template on to thin cream card twice, then cut them out.

2 Cut two strips of card, 5 cm x 30cm. Glue the headband pieces together to make one long strip.

3 Measure the headband to fit, then glue or tape the ends together.

4 Copy or trace the smaller inner ear template on to thin white card twice, then cut them out. Stick them on to the main ear pieces. Glue the two rabbit ears on to the middle of the headband. Squeak!

You will need:
* Thin cream and white card
* Scissors
* PVA glue

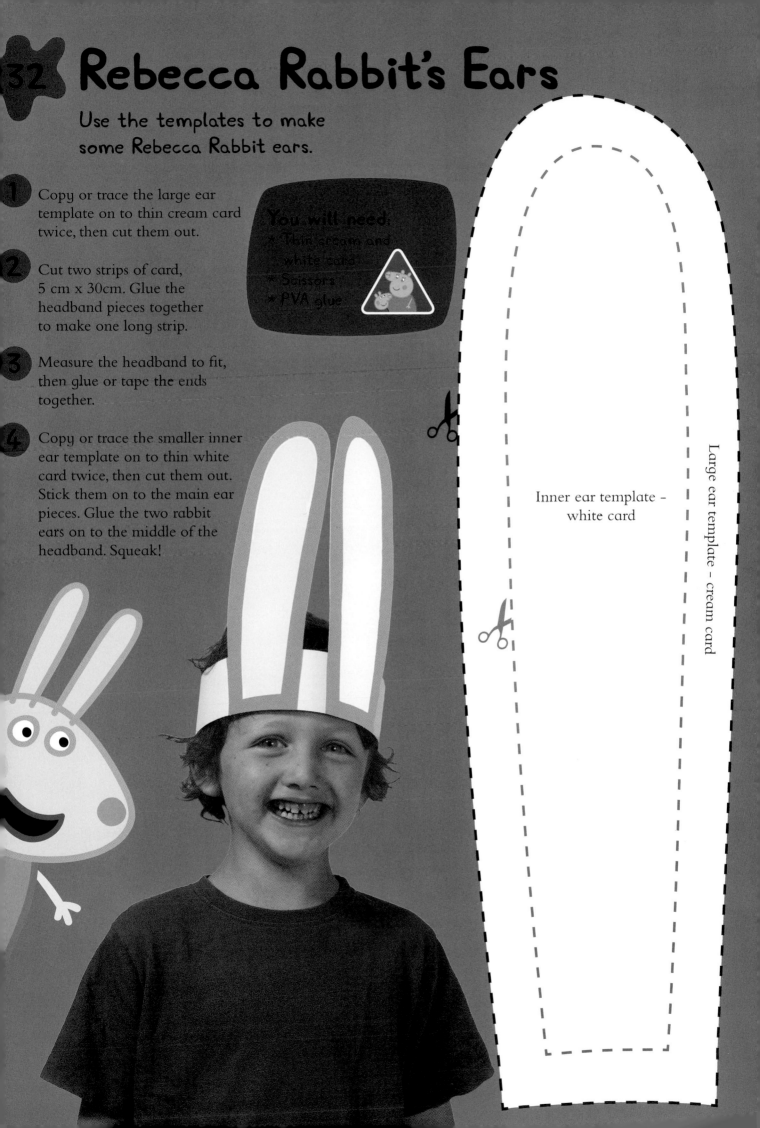

Inner ear template – white card

Large ear template – cream card

Miss Rabbit's Carrot Cake

Do you know Miss Rabbit's favourite cake? It's carrot, of course – with some tasty marzipan carrots on the top!

You will need:
* 125g self-raising flour
* 125g plain flour
* 1 tsp bicarbonate of soda
* 2 tsp ground cinnamon
* 1 tsp ground ginger
* 250ml vegetable oil
* 190g soft brown sugar
* 4 eggs
* 175g golden syrup
* 400g grated carrot
* 60g pecans, chopped
* 5 tbsp honey
* 23cm cake tin
* Baking paper
* Cocktail stick

To decorate:
* 100g unsalted butter, softened
* 2 tsp orange extract
* 100g cream cheese
* 125g icing sugar
* Marzipan
* Orange and green food colouring

Delicious!

1 Preheat the oven to 160°C (gas mark 3). Lightly grease the cake tin and line with baking paper.

2 Sift together the self-raising flour, plain flour, bicarbonate of soda, cinnamon and ginger in a bowl.

3 Whisk the oil, sugar, eggs and syrup in another bowl. Add to the flour mixture and stir well.

4 Stir in the grated carrot and nuts. Spoon into the cake tin, then bake for 1¼–1½ hours until golden.

5 Remove the cake from the oven and poke a few little holes in the top with a wooden kebab stick.

6 Drizzle over the honey, then leave the cake to cool in the tin while you make the icing.

7 Beat together the butter, orange extract and cream cheese, then mix in the icing sugar.

8 Remove the cake from the tin, slice it in half and add a layer of icing. Put some more icing on top.

9 Colour most of your marzipan orange with 1–2 drops of orange food colouring and roll into carrot shapes. Colour the rest of the marzipan green to make the leaves. Add two long green leaves to each carrot. Munch! Munch! Very tasty!

Rebecca Rabbit likes carrot cake, too!

34 Indoor Den

When it's cold outside, have fun making an indoor den. Drape blankets and sheets over furniture and fill your den with cushions and blankets.

35 Memory Game

One person chooses 8–10 everyday things (such as a teaspoon, a pencil or a tiny toy) and arranges them on a tray. Everyone then has 30 seconds to look at the things on the tray before they are covered up. Who can remember the most things?

36 Treasure Hunt

Get someone like Mummy Pig or Daddy Pig to hide some treasure, then have fun looking for it! The treasure could be a chocolate coin or a small toy.

IN THE HALL
Above the boots, below the hat is where you'll find this clue is at!

IN THE KITCHEN
Find a dish that's red and blue, and look . . . you'll see another clue!

Make it more difficult by having clues, so one clue leads to another clue, and then that clue leads to another clue, so it takes longer to find the treasure.

37 Muddy Puddles Game

Splat! Here's a muddy puddles game you can play indoors!

1 Cut some big puddle shapes out of thick brown cardboard and attach them to the floor with reusable adhesive. There should be one puddle fewer than the number of players.

2 Dance round the puddles while some music is playing.

3 When the music stops, jump on to a puddle. There should only be one person on each puddle.

4 The player who doesn't jump on to a puddle in time is out of the game. Remove a puddle and start again.

5 The winner is the first person to jump on to the last puddle when the music stops.

Jumping in muddy puddles is Peppa's favourite thing to do!

38 Balloon Race

Have a balloon race! Each person puts a balloon between their knees and races across the room. How fast can you go without dropping the balloon?

39 Balloon Keepie-uppie

Blow up some balloons. How long can you keep tapping your balloon to keep it in the air? Who can keep their balloon in the air the longest?

Knight's Helmet

Look! It's Brave Sir George! Here's how to make a helmet fit for a fairy-tale knight.

You will need:
* Cardboard
* Card
* Scissors
* Masking tape
* Silver foil
* Feathers (red and yellow)
* Split pins
* Sticky tape

1

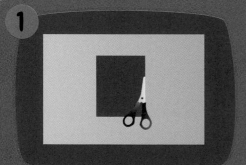

Cut out a piece of cardboard wide enough to fit around your head and long enough to reach from the top of your head to your shoulders. Cut a large square from the centre of the cardboard for your face.

2

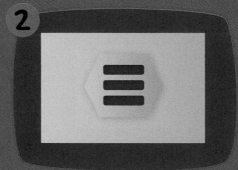

Taking a piece of card, cut out a grille shape slightly larger than the square hole, with slits to see through. Cover it in silver foil.

3

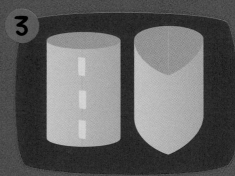

Roll the large piece of cardboard into a cylinder shape, and tape the ends together. Make a fold down the opposite side of the helmet to the tape so the front of the helmet comes out into a point.

4

Cut out a teardrop-shaped piece of cardboard to fit the top of the helmet, cover the helmet and the teardrop shape in foil, then tape them together.

5

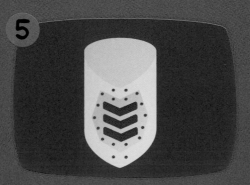

Attach the grille over the outside of the hole with a row of split pins to look like rivets. Bend back the arms of the split pins inside the helmet.

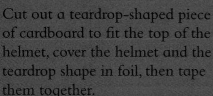
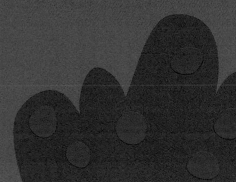

Brave Sir George's Shield

If Brave Sir George is going to chase away the scary green dragon, he'll need a shield! Here's how to make one.

Put your arm through the handle at the back of the shield to hold the shield in front of your body.

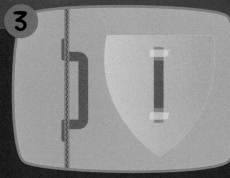

1

Cut two shield-shaped pieces of corrugated card from a large cardboard box.

2

Cut a long slot in the centre of one piece of cardboard measuring 15cm x 3cm.

3

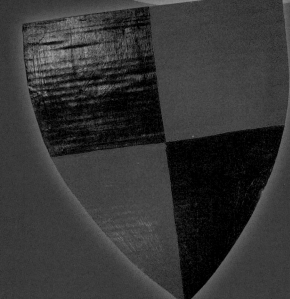

Cut a strip of card measuring 30cm x 2.5cm. Push the card through the slot and tape down the edges, as shown.

4

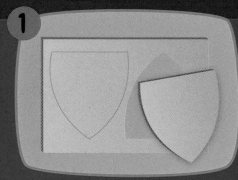

Glue the two parts of the shield together, so the cardboard handle is sticking out of the back on the outside.

5

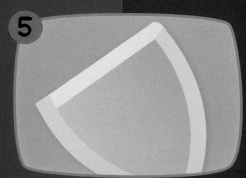

Cover the rough edges round the outside of the shield with masking tape, then paint the whole shield yellow.

6

When dry, divide the shield into quarters with a ruler and pencil, then paint the two opposite quarters red.

Once Upon a Time . . .

Look! Her Royal Highness Princess Peppa is having
a picnic in the clouds with Brave Sir George. Oh no!
What's that terrible roar? It's a scary green dragon . . .

Make up an exciting story about
what happens when Peppa and
George come face to face with
the scary green dragon!

43 Hubble Bubble

Here's how to make your own mixture to make lots and lots of bubbles.

You will need:
* Large bowl
* Washing-up liquid
* Bottle of glycerin (from pharmacy, optional)
* Water
* Wire coathanger

1 Mix together equal amounts of washing-up liquid, water and glycerin, if you have it.

2 Pour the mixture in a deep, wide bowl, such as a washing-up bowl.

3 Bend a wire coathanger into a circle, dip it in the bubble mixture . . . and wave it around!

Peppa and George LOVE blowing bubbles! How big is the biggest bubble you can blow?

Glycerin is not essential, but will make your bubbles stronger!

Bubble Paintings

If you like blowing bubbles, why not print some colourful bubble patterns!

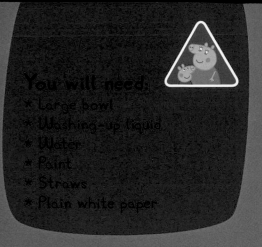

1

Mix paints, water and a squirt of washing-up liquid in a bowl.

2

Blow air into the mixture through a straw to make lots of bubbles.

3

Gently rest a sheet of plain paper on top to make a bubble print.

45 Salt-dough Beads

These pretty salt-dough beads can be strung into a bracelet or a necklace.

You will need: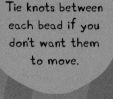
* Salt dough
* Wooden kebab skewers
* Poster paints
* PVA glue
* Water
* Ribbon

Thread beads on to a long piece of ribbon.

See Make 24 for how to make and bake salt dough and Make 46 for how to varnish.

Tie knots between each bead if you don't want them to move.

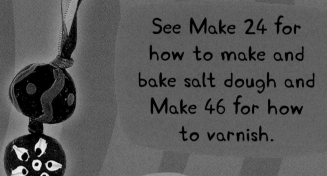

1

Roll the salt dough into a long sausage then break it into smaller chunks so the beads are roughly the same size.

2

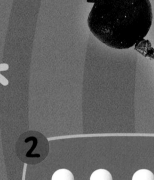

Roll each piece of dough into a ball between the palms of your hand.

3

Gently push a wooden kebab skewer through the beads to make holes big enough to push ribbon or thread through. Make sure the holes are quite large as the dough may spread slightly in cooking.

4 Remove the skewers and bake the beads until the dough has gone hard.

5 When cool, paint the beads with brightly coloured poster paints, then varnish them.

You will need about 20 beads to make one necklace.

Mini Bug Bookmarks

Fix ribbons on to tiny balls of salt dough to make these colourful bug bookmarks!

You will need:
* Salt dough
* Paints
* Paintbrush
* Green ribbon
* PVA glue
* Water
* Pinking shears
* White tissue paper

1 Model bugs out of salt dough, then bake following the instructions in Make 24.

2 Paint the bugs bright colours, then glue them on to the ends of long green ribbons.

3 Cut the ends of the ribbons with pinking shears so they don't fray.

If you varnish your bug bookmarks, they will last longer!

Layer white tissue paper with PVA glue. Once dry, cut out some wings.

Salt-dough varnish:
- Mix one part PVA glue to three parts water.
- Cover each model with the mixture when the paint is dry. (The mixture looks milky at first but dries clear and hard.)

47 Pom-pom Chick

You can make lots of different animals when you know how to make a pom-pom. Here's how to make a little yellow chick.

You will need:
* Card
* Scissors
* Ruler
* Compass and pencil
* Yellow wool
* Googly eyes
* Yellow and orange felt
* PVA glue

Cut out yellow felt wings and glue them on.

1

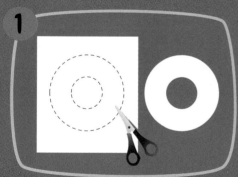

Fold a piece of card in half. Draw an 8cm-wide circle with a 5cm-wide circle inside it.

2

Cut out both the large circles and the inner circles to make two doughnut shapes.

3

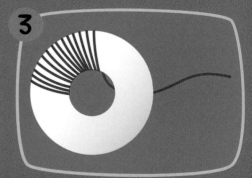

Put the two circles together. Wrap wool round them until a tiny hole is left in the centre.

4

Snip the wool round the edge. Keep snipping until you reach the card circles inside.

5

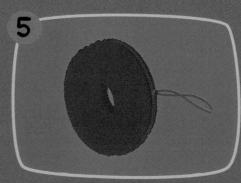

Tie a length of wool between the pieces of card and knot, to keep the wool together.

6

Remove the card, trim the wool into a neat ball, then cut out and glue on orange felt pieces for the beak and feet, and add googly eyes.

48 Pom-pom Ice Creams

Turn some pom-poms into these tasty-looking ice creams!

You will need: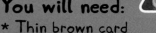
* Thin brown card
* Pencil
* Scissors
* Large plate
* Various colours of wool
* PVA glue

1 Follow instructions 1–5 opposite to make a pom-pom. Use a different colour of wool for each flavour.

2 Remove the card circles and trim the wool into a neat ball.

3 Place the plate on the card and draw around it. Cut out the circle.

4 Fold the circle in half, then in half again, then cut along the folds.

5 Take one of the quarter circles and curve it into a cone shape. Glue it in place, then pop an ice-cream pom-pom on top!

★ **Peppa's Ice Creams** ★

open

Strawberry

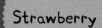

Vanilla

Chocolate

Pirate Card

Shiver me timbers! This birthday card is perfect for anyone who loves pirates!

You will need:
* Coloured card
* White card for stencil
* Scissors
* Paints
* Sponge

1 Copy or trace the skull and crossbones template on to card and cut it out.

2 Hold the stencil over a piece of card and dab paint through it with a sponge.

3 Let the paint dry before writing your card.

Happy Birthday, Danny Dog!

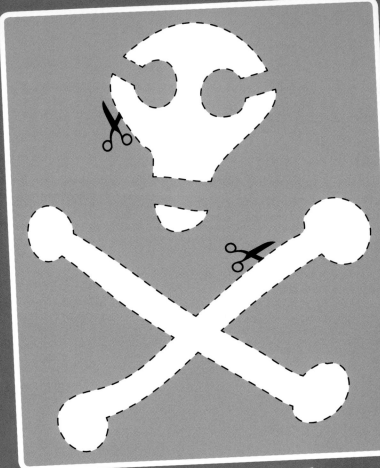

Danny Dog's Pirate Hat

A-harrr!

You will need:
* A2 black sugar paper
* Sticky tape or glue
* Pirate stencil
* White poster paint
* Sponge

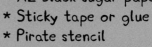
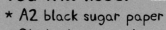
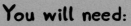

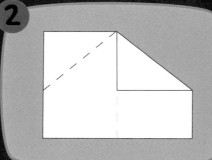

Dab white paint over the pirate stencil with a sponge to add this scary skull and crossbones on the front of the hat.

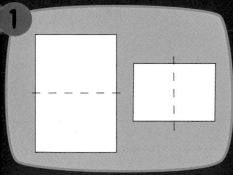

1 Fold a piece of black paper in half, then in half again. Open out the second fold.

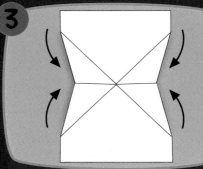

2 Fold down the top corners, as shown, then fold them back the opposite way.

3 Open out the paper slightly, then push the corners down inside the folds.

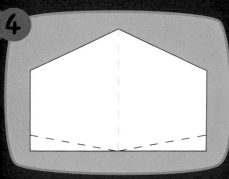

4 Fold the bottom edges up at each side, as shown. Turn over and repeat the same folds on the other side to match.

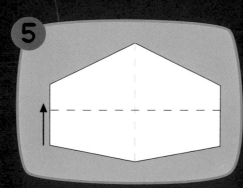

5 Fold the paper up at the front. Turn over and repeat on the back to match.

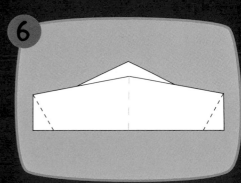

6 Fold back the corners at each side of the hat on the front and back. Tuck the folds inside and glue or tape them together.

Treasure Cup

This gleaming golden cup makes perfect pirate treasure!

You will need:
* Oval balloon
* Old newspaper
* PVA glue
* Water
* Card
* Scissors
* Compass
* Pencil
* Cardboard tube
* String
* Gold or silver paint
* Paintbrush
* Stick-on gems
* Sticky tape
* Safety pin

1

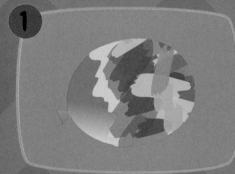

Blow up a balloon and cover half of it in 5–6 layers of papier mâché. Pop the balloon with a safety pin when dry.

2

Cut out a circle of card, make a slit from the edge to the centre, and tape it into a cone shape.

3

Push the cone inside a cardboard tube and tape the tube to the bottom of the papier mâché bowl.

4

Make sure the cup can stand up, then cover the base in 3–4 layers of papier mâché.

5

Cut out two strips of card and tape to the sides of the bowl to make handles. Cover in papier mâché.

6

Trim the top of the bowl with scissors and glue strips of paper over the edge to neaten it.

 7 Glue string around the stem and bowl of the treasure cup to make a raised pattern.

 8 When the glue is dry, paint the cup silver or gold, and add some shiny stick-on gems.

See Make 5 for how to make papier mâché.

52 Paper Boat

Make a paper boat from a sheet of A4 paper!

1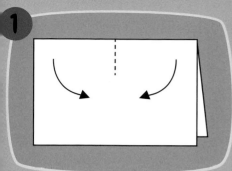

Fold the paper in half, then make a crease in the centre, at the top.

2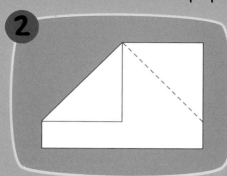

Fold down each corner towards the middle.

3

Fold the edges of the paper up on both sides, then open out the paper in a hat shape.

4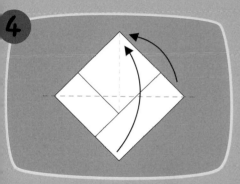

Bring the corners of the hat towards each other and flatten the shape into a square.

5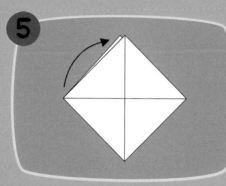

Hold the open corners of the square and fold each one up, to make flattened triangles as shown in the drawing in step 6.

6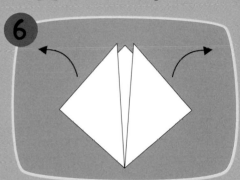

Flatten the triangle into a square by opening it up in the middle to fold the two bottom corners together and fold flat into a square.

7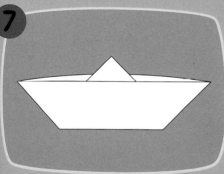

Gently pull the sides of the triangle out to make a boat shape.

53 Make Up a Pirate Story

Shiver me timbers! Captain George and Pirate Peppa have followed a treasure map all the way to a desert island. They start to dig in the sand for buried treasure when suddenly some more pirates arrive . . .
Make up a story about what happens next.

54 Treasure Map

Why not make a secret treasure map showing where you plan to bury some pirate treasure?

55 Treasure-map Case

Next, make this case to keep your treasure map safe!

You will need:
* Long snack tube with a lid
* Thin brown card
* Split pins
* Rope or thick string
* PVA glue
* Black tape or card
* Scissors

1

Wrap and glue brown card around the tube and cut out a circle to stick on the lid.

2

Glue a long piece of thick string to the sides of the tube at the top.

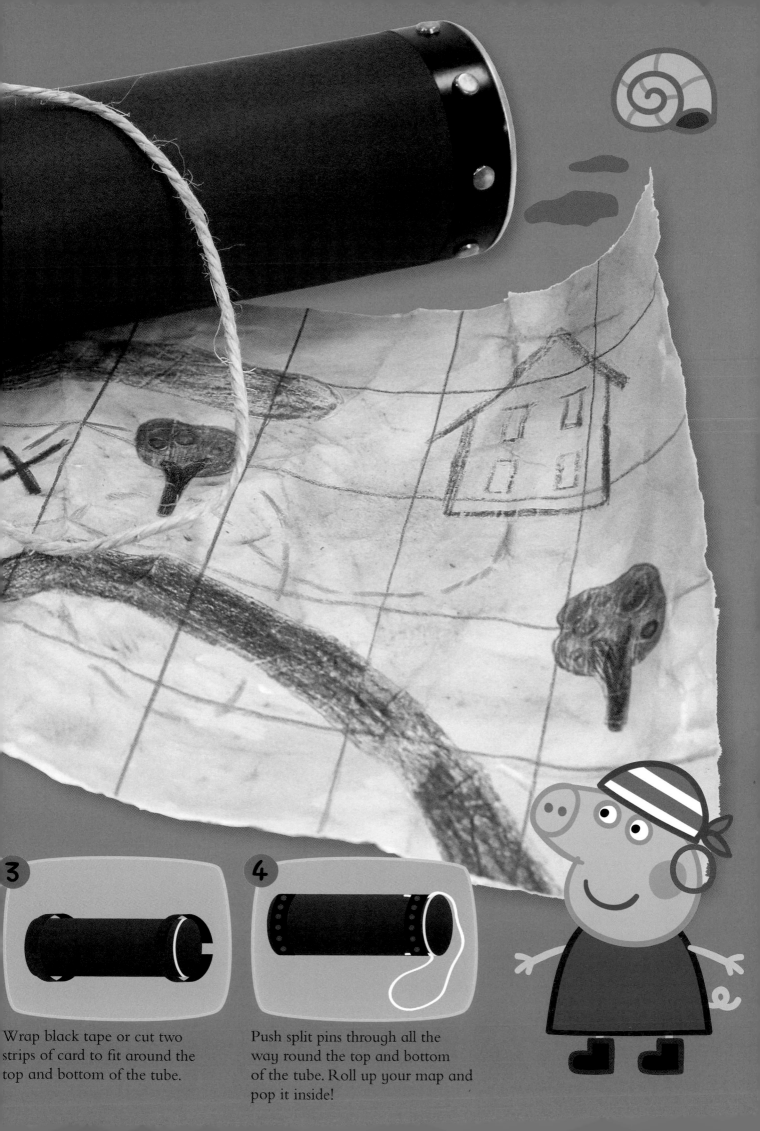

3 Wrap black tape or cut two strips of card to fit around the top and bottom of the tube.

4 Push split pins through all the way round the top and bottom of the tube. Roll up your map and pop it inside!

Treasure Chest

Every pirate needs a chest to store his or her treasure in . . .

You will need:
* Large shoebox with lid
* Brown card
* Pencil
* PVA glue
* Brown and black paints
* Paintbrush
* Old comb or brush
* Black tape or card
* Gold card
* Split pins
* Plate
* Scissors

Add black card straps studded with split pins.

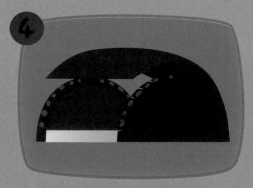

1 Cut out a piece of brown card, long enough to curve over the top of your shoebox lid to make a dome shape.

2 Draw around a plate that's the same width as the shoebox lid on to more brown card. Then draw a bigger circle (1.5cm wider) around the first circle. Cut around the bigger circle, then cut it in half.

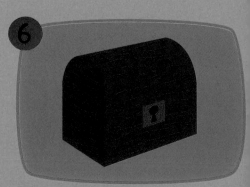

3 Snip around the edges of the semicircles to the inner line, then fold the flaps over. Glue the semicircles to either side of the lid along the flat edges.

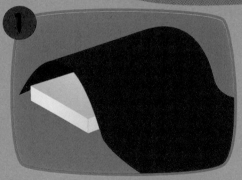

4 Glue the long piece of brown card over the top, curving the card and sticking it to the flaps on both sides as you go along.

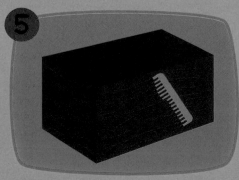

5 Cover the base of the shoebox in brown card. Drag black paint into lines with the teeth of an old comb to look like wood.

6 Cut a keyhole shape out of black card and stick it on to a square piece of gold card. Glue it on to the front of the shoebox.

Captain Peppa Says . . .

Decide who is going to be Captain Peppa
and play this simple game with
your shipmates!

Captain Peppa tells
all the other players what to
do, but they must only do things
that start with the command,
"Captain Peppa says."

If Captain Peppa says, "Captain Peppa
says touch your toes," you must do it.

But if she only says, "Touch your
toes," and you do it, you will
be out of the game.

58 Mr Potato

Make your very own Mr Potato!

You will need:
* Big potato
* Scissors
* Black and red card
* Brown and yellow felt
* PVA glue
* Cloves
* Pipe cleaners

1. Choose a big potato to be your Mr Potato.

2. Use the template to make his hat from felt and glue the felt pieces on to a piece of card to make it sturdy.

3. Poke cloves into the potato to make Mr Potato's eyes and use the templates to make his smiley mouth and moustache from card, then stick them on.

Now make Mr Potato's car on the next page!

Push in pipe cleaners for his hands and feet.

hat template

moustache and mouth templates

59 Mr Potato's Car

Mr Potato has come to town! Make his car from papier mâché and an old plastic drinks bottle.

You will need:
* Sausage-shaped balloon
* Newspaper
* PVA glue
* Water
* Large plastic drinks bottle
* Scissors
* Cardboard (red, yellow and black)
* Poster paint
* Paintbrush
* Cocktail sticks
* Safety pin

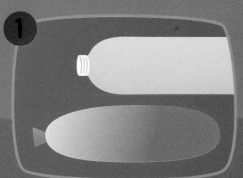

Blow up a sausage-shaped balloon so it's the same width as the bottle.

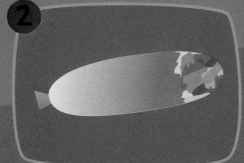

Cover the rounded end of the balloon with 3–4 layers of papier mâché.

Use lots of papier mâché to build up the sides to form the car shape.

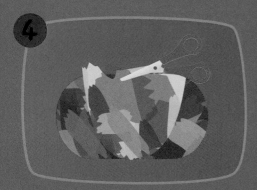

Pop the balloon with a safety pin when the glue is dry. Cut the edge and glue over strips of paper to make it neat.

Leave the car to dry, then paint it red. Glue on four black cardboard wheels, a stripy grille and two yellow headlights.

Copying the shape in the picture opposite, cut out a red rotor and fix it into the top of the bottle with a cocktail stick.

Cut a round steering wheel out of black cardboard and stick it to a cocktail stick. Glue the cocktail stick to the floor of the car so Mr Potato can steer!

Slide the bottle carefully over Mr Potato so he's ready to drive away!

See Make 5 for how to make papier mâché.

60 Sun Wall Hanging

Make this bright yellow sun to hang on your wall!

What you need:
* Salt dough
* Large and small plates
* Rolling pin
* Water
* Paintbrush
* Blunt knife
* Pencil
* Small metal hook
* Paint

1

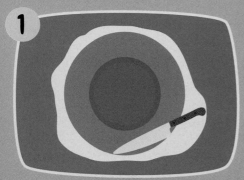

Roll out some salt dough, then ask an adult to help you cut round a large plate to make a circle.

2

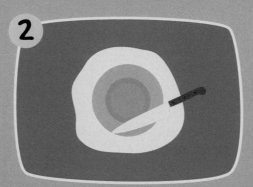

Roll out some more salt dough, then cut round a small plate to make a smaller circle.

3

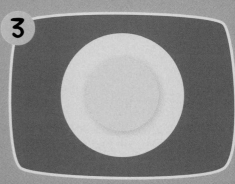

Wet one side of the small circle with water and stick it to the middle of the large circle.

4

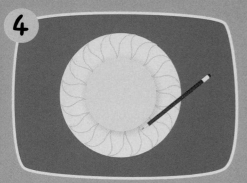

Make the shape of the sun's rays in the dough with a pencil and ask an adult to cut them out.

5

Bake your sun in the oven. Leave to cool, then paint it in bright sunshine colours. Attach the metal hook to the back of your sun to hang it on the wall.

See Make 24 for how to make and bake salt dough and Make 46 for the varnish.

61 Rainmaker

Tip this instrument from side to side to make a swooshing sound like falling rain!

You will need:
* Long cardboard snack tube with a lid
* Silver foil
* Dried rice, lentils or peas
* Craft foam or cardboard
* Coloured or white paper
* Paints
* Paintbrush
* Scissors
* PVA glue
* Decorations

1. Gather and twist a sheet of silver foil into a spiral and put it inside the tube.

2. Fill the tube a quarter full of dried rice, lentils or peas, then put on the lid.

3. Cover your tube in coloured or white paper, then paint your rainmaker bright colours. Glue on some craft foam shapes, glittery sequins or craft feathers.

If your tube doesn't have a lid, tape some paper over the ends.

Remove some foil if the rice or peas get stuck, or add more if they whizz down the tube too fast and you want to slow them down.

Tip or shake the instrument to hear the swooshing sound.

A Rainy-day Walk

Put on your raincoat and some wellington boots, then go for a walk in the rain. Have fun splashing in all the puddles!

See how many of these things you can find on your walk in the rain:

* Grey clouds
* Slugs or snails
* A wiggly worm
* A muddy puddle
* A rainbow

63 Weather Watch

What's the weather like today? Make a weather chart to see how the weather changes where you live.

You will need:
* Large sheet of paper
* Felt-tip pens or coloured pencils
* Ruler

1 Divide the paper into boxes, one for every day of the week or month.

2 Write the days of the week along the top of the calendar.

3 Make up some little pictures to show all the different kinds of weather . . .

4 . . . then draw a picture to show what the weather is like every day!

Monday	Tuesday	Wednesday	Thursday	Friday	Saturday	Sunday
1	2	3	4	5	6	7
8	9	10	11	12	13	14
15	16	17	18	19	20	21
22	23	24	25	26	27	28
29	30	31				

Peppa likes rainy days because then you get MUDDY PUDDLES! Snort!

64 Rainbow and Clouds

Make this hanging cloud and rainbow
to remind you of your rainy-day walk!

You will need:
* Paper plate
* Cotton-wool balls
* PVA glue
* Paintbrush
* Tissue paper in all the
  colours of the rainbow!
* Ribbon

1 Fold the paper plate in half
and glue it together.

2 Paint on PVA glue with a
brush and cover the plate
with balls of cotton wool
to make a cloud.

3 Cut strips of tissue paper in
various colours so they are all
the same length, and glue them
on to the back of the plate.

4 Stick a loop of ribbon to the top
of the cloud to hang up your rainbow.

Put the strips in order so
they match the colours
of the rainbow.
The order is:
* red
* orange
* yellow
* green
* blue
* indigo
* violet

65 Shadow Tag

On a sunny day, try to "tag" someone
by stepping on his or her shadow.

The person chasing everyone else's
shadows is "it". If he or she steps
on someone's shadow, then that
person becomes "it" instead!

Hot-air Balloon

Up, up and away! Make this colourful hot-air balloon to hang from your ceiling!

1

Blow up an oval balloon and cover three quarters of it in 5-6 layers of papier mâché. When dry, pop the balloon with a safety pin and remove it.

2

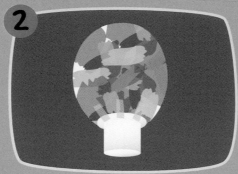

Cut a large yoghurt pot in half. Tape the top half of the yoghurt pot to the balloon, as shown, and cover both parts of the yoghurt pot in 3–4 layers of papier mâché.

3

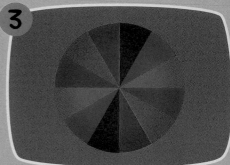

Divide the balloon into 12 sections and paint them different colours. Paint the other half of the yoghurt pot to look like a basket.

4

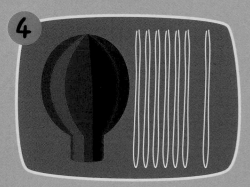

Measure a piece of string from the top of the balloon to the bottom and then double it. Cut 7 pieces of string this length.

5

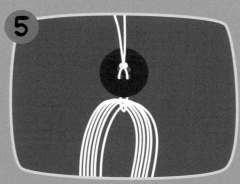

Place 6 of the strings together and fold them in half. Tie the seventh piece of string around the halfway point. Thread the button on to the tied string and knot it in place.

6

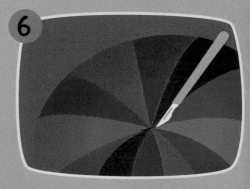

Cut a tiny slit at the very top of the balloon using a craft knife. The slit should just be big enough to push the edge of the button through.

7

Holding all of the strands, slide the button into the slit so it twists into place and can't be pulled out.

8

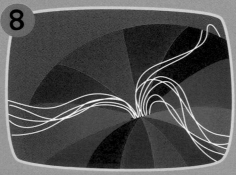

Hold the two strands attached to the button together to keep them out of the way. These will be the hanging strings for your balloon when finished.

9

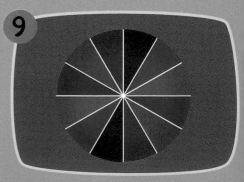

Carefully position each of the other strands equally around the balloon to divide the colour sections.

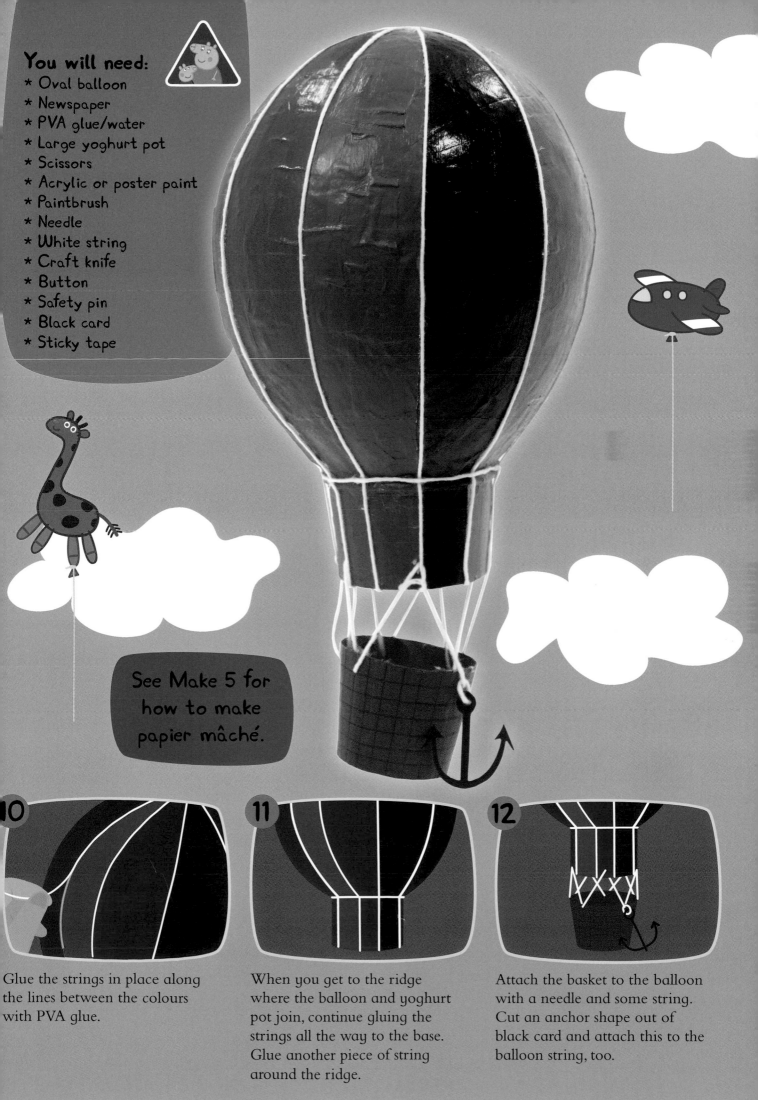

You will need:
* Oval balloon
* Newspaper
* PVA glue/water
* Large yoghurt pot
* Scissors
* Acrylic or poster paint
* Paintbrush
* Needle
* White string
* Craft knife
* Button
* Safety pin
* Black card
* Sticky tape

See Make 5 for how to make papier mâché.

10

Glue the strings in place along the lines between the colours with PVA glue.

11

When you get to the ridge where the balloon and yoghurt pot join, continue gluing the strings all the way to the base. Glue another piece of string around the ridge.

12

Attach the basket to the balloon with a needle and some string. Cut an anchor shape out of black card and attach this to the balloon string, too.

Fridge Magnets

These little cars and trains have magnets on the back so you can stick them on the front of your fridge!

You will need:
* Salt dough
* Paints
* PVA glue
* Water
* Tiny magnets

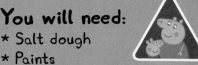

Shape cars, trucks and trains out of salt dough. Bake the models and leave to cool. Paint in bright colours and glue a tiny magnet on to the back of each model.

Paint on a coat of PVA glue mixed with water to "varnish" the models (see Make 46).

Peppa says . . .

If you make enough vehicles, you can have a traffic jam on your fridge door!

See Make 24 for how to make and bake salt dough.

Printing Fun

Have fun printing using all sorts of everyday things found around the house.

You will need:
* Paper   * PVA glue
* Thick paint   * Objects to
* Corks   print with!

Try printing with:
• Buttons
• Coins
• Dried pasta shapes
• Wooden paintbrush ends
• Old keys
• Cookie cutters

Glue buttons and other small objects on to corks or small pieces of wood to make them easier to print with.

69 Fingerprint Flowers

You can also print with your fingers! Paint this lovely flower with your fingertips.

You will need:
* Plain paper
* Coloured paper
* Paints
* Corrugated cardboard
* PVA glue
* Scissors
* Your fingers!

Print the stem with the edge of a piece of corrugated cardboard dipped in paint. Make the flowers by printing lots of colourful dots in circles with the tip of your finger.

Cut a vase shape out of coloured paper and glue it over the stems.

70 Fingerprint Animals

Print lots of little animal prints using your fingers and thumbs!

Buzzy bees

Dip your thumb in yellow paint and press it on to a piece of paper to paint the body. When dry, draw on stripes, legs and wings with a black felt-tip pen. Then draw on an eye or glue on a tiny googly eye instead.

Ants

Make three black blobs with different-sized fingers. Draw on antennae and legs when the paint is dry and glue on googly eyes.

Frogs

Make a green blob with your thumb or fingertip. When the paint is dry, draw on a mouth and legs, and glue on two googly eyes.

71 Peppa's Photo Album

Here's Peppa's photo album, full of pictures of her family and friends. Why not make one, too?

1 Cut out two equal-sized pieces of cardboard. Glue them on the back of your sheet of wrapping paper, leaving a narrow gap in between them.

2 Cut round the wrapping paper so it is 2cm–3cm bigger than the cardboard. Fold down the edges of the paper and glue them on to the cardboard.

3 Tape together lots of sheets of paper and fold them into a concertina to make your photo album's pages. (See the next page for how to make a concertina.)

4 Glue one piece of ribbon to the inside edge of the front cover and one to the inside edge of the back cover, then glue in your pages.

Peppa's Photos

You will need:
* Scissors
* Coloured cardboard
* Brightly coloured wrapping paper
* PVA glue
* Sticky tape
* Plain or coloured paper
* Two lengths of ribbon
* Stick-on gems
* Photographs!

Use stick-on gems, rolled-up swirls of paper, pictures or anything else you like to decorate the front cover. Now you are ready to stick your photos inside!

See Make 2 for a Peppa template to trace and colour for your cover.

George

Suzy Sheep

dfish

To make a concertina:

1

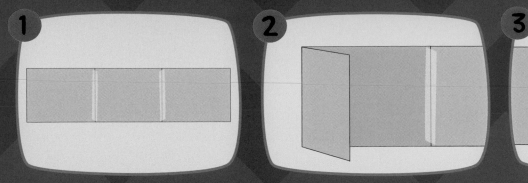

Tape some sheets of A4 paper together to make one long strip of paper.

2

Fold the edge of the paper over, to the size you want your book page to be.

3

Turn the strip of paper over and fold the paper back on top of the first fold.

4

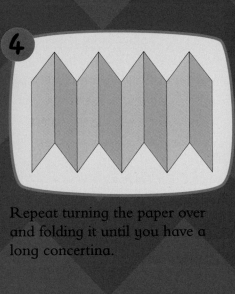

Repeat turning the paper over and folding it until you have a long concertina.

Sweet Dishes

These little sweet dishes are made out of papier mâché covered in layers of colourful tissue paper.

You will need:
* Saucer
* Cling film
* Old newspaper
* PVA glue
* Water
* Scissors
* Tissue paper

1

Wrap a piece of cling film over a saucer. (This will stop the papier mâché from sticking.)

2

Cover the face of the saucer with four layers of papier mâché, then leave to dry.

3

Peel your dry paper dish off the saucer, then cut around the edge, to neaten.

4

Cover both sides of your dish in strips of brightly coloured tissue paper. Glue on 3–4 layers of tissue paper so you cannot see the newspaper underneath.

See Make 5 for how to make papier mâché.

73 Papier Mâché Piggy Bank

Save your pennies in this papier mâché piggy bank!

You will need:
* Oval or round balloon
* Old newspapers
* PVA glue
* Water
* Card
* Masking tape
* Pipe cleaner
* Scissors
* Poster paint
* Paintbrush
* Yoghurt pot
* Pin

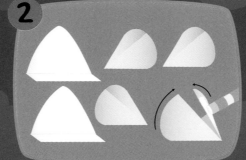

1

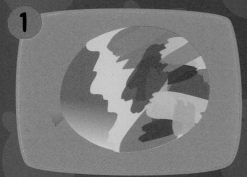

Blow up the balloon, and cover it in five layers of papier mâché, leaving a small area around the knot uncovered. Then leave to dry.

2

Cut two ear shapes from card. Cut two circles of card in half, then glue into cones to make the legs.

3

Ask an adult to burst and remove the balloon, then tape the legs, ears and yoghurt-pot snout on to your pig's body.

4

Ask an adult to make a hole in the back with a pin. Push in a curly pipe-cleaner tail.

5

Cover the ears, legs, snout and tail with two layers of papier mâché, and leave to dry.

6

Ask an adult to cut a slit in the top for your pennies, then paint your papier mâché piggy!

Make sure the papier mâché is completely dry before painting – this can take 2–3 days!

Hop-hop-hopscotch

Peppa and her friends love playing hopscotch.
Chalk a grid on a safe driveway, pavement
or in a playground and have a game, too.

You will need:
* Chalk
* Small, smooth pebbles
* Your hopping and jumping skills!

Make each box about 30cm square.

1 Chalk out your hopscotch grid, copying the picture above. Then take turns throwing your pebbles on to the squares.

2 To start, throw your pebble into square 1. Jump over the stone, landing with both feet on squares 2 and 3. Then hop on to square 4 and jump with both feet on squares 5 and 6. Next, hop on square 7, jump with both feet on squares 8 and 9, then hop on to square 10.

3 Hop round to face the opposite way, then jump and hop back, picking up your pebble from square 1 as you go.

4 Next, throw your pebble so it lands inside square 2 and carry on jumping and hopping up and down the hopscotch grid.

5 Miss a go if you don't throw your stone into the correct square, or if you step on a chalk line.

75 Skip-skip-skipping

Find a skipping rope and see how many jumps you can
do in one go. Can you get to 10 or 20 or even more?

76 Piggy in the Middle

To play Piggy in the Middle, two people throw a ball to each other while someone in the middle tries to catch it. If the piggy in the middle catches the ball, then the person who threw it becomes the "piggy" instead.

77 Jump in a Muddy Puddle!

Everyone loves to jump in muddy puddles! Put on your wellington boots and jump in muddy puddles, just like Peppa and George!

Throw the Wellie

Take turns playing Throw the Wellie into a circle. You could use hula hoops or draw chalk circles on the ground. Write numbers inside the circles. Everyone playing takes turns to throw their wellie so it lands inside each circle. Add up the points as you go round the course. The player with the most points wins!

Sack Race

Find some old pillowcases or sacks and have a sack race. Each person steps inside their pillowcase or sack, holds it up with their hands, and jumps! Who'll be the first to jump past the finish line?

You will need:
* Apples
* Apple corer
* Knife
* Lemon juice
* Water
* Baking sheet

1 **2** **3**

If you like the taste, you can sprinkle your apple slices with cinnamon before they go in the oven.

81 Grow a Sunflower

Grow a sunflower in your garden or in a large pot on a balcony.

You will need:
* Packet of sunflower seeds
* Patch of flowerbed or a large flower pot and some potting compost
* Bamboo cane
* Garden twine
* Pencil

1 Put a bamboo cane in a flowerbed or large pot filled with potting compost. Make a hole in the soil with a pencil.

2 Put 2–3 seeds in the hole and cover them with soil.

3 Water the soil and wait for your sunflowers to grow.

4 As each plant grows, tie its stem to the cane with garden twine.

Harvesting your sunflower seeds
Sunflower seeds are ready to harvest when the backs of the flowers turn yellowy brown and start to droop.

Cut off the flowers and hang them up to dry or put them in a paper bag. Once dry, the seeds will fall out of the flower head. If your sunflower has edible seeds, wash the seeds before you eat them.

If you like, you can roast your sunflower seeds by spreading them on a baking sheet and placing it in the oven for around 45 minutes at 140°C. Stir the seeds occasionally as they cook.

Store the seeds in an airtight container.

Choose easy-to-grow sunflowers with seeds you can eat.

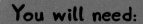

Trail Mix

Make a tasty trail mix to munch on next time you go for a walk!

Mix cupfuls of your favourite ingredients in a big bowl. Store the mixture in an airtight container until your next walk, then divide the trail mix into paper bags, one for each person. You could even add the dried apple opposite to the mix!

Here are some things to try:
- Sunflower seeds
- Chopped nuts such as hazelnuts or pecans
- Raisins
- Chocolate chips
- Dried banana chips
- Dried coconut chips

83

Robot George

Look at George dressed as a robot! Here's how to make a robot costume, too.

You will need:
* Large cardboard box
* Small cardboard box
* Scissors
* Silver foil
* Coloured card
* Plastic bottle tops
* PVA glue
* 2 green pipe cleaners
* Black wool

1 Check the boxes to make sure there are no staples or sharp edges inside.

2 Remove or tape up any loose flaps.

3

Try the large box on for size, then ask a grown-up to cut armholes for you in each side and a square at the top for your head to go through. Then cut a large square in the front of the small box so you can see out.

4

Glue shiny silver foil all over the boxes and decorate with glued-on bottle tops and shapes cut out of coloured card.

Glue a black pom-pom on to a green pipe cleaner to make an antenna. Make two of these and glue them on to the robot's head.

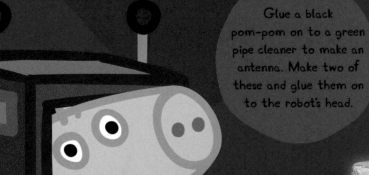

See Make 47 for how to make a pop-pom.

85 Time Capsule

Fill a metal box with things about you and your family, then hide it somewhere safe.

Things to include:
* Photographs
* Drawings
* Birthday cards
* Tickets to a favourite place
* A little toy
* Favourite jokes
* Songs recorded on a memory stick

Tape the lid shut and write a message on the lid that your time capsule is not to be opened for five, 10 or even 15 years!

Hide your time capsule in a safe place but don't forget where you put it! Hee Hee!

Finger Puppet

Here's how to make a little card finger puppet that looks just like Candy Cat's tiger!

You will need:
* Thin card
* Scissors
* Sticky tape
* PVA glue
* Coloured pens or pencils

1 Copy or trace the templates on to thin card, then colour them in.

2 Roll the body shape into a cone. Tape or glue along the edge.

3 Cut out the head and tail and glue on to the cone.

templates

Colour in the stripes.

Give Candy Cat's tiger a smiley face!

Meow!

87 Eggbox Tortoise

This little eggbox tortoise looks
just like Dr Hamster's Tiddles!

You will need:
* Card
* Scissors
* Cardboard eggbox
* PVA glue
* Paint
* Paintbrush
* Googly eyes

1 Copy or trace the template
on to green card or plain card
painted green, and cut out.

2 Tear out the compartment of a
cardboard eggbox and paint it
pale brown.

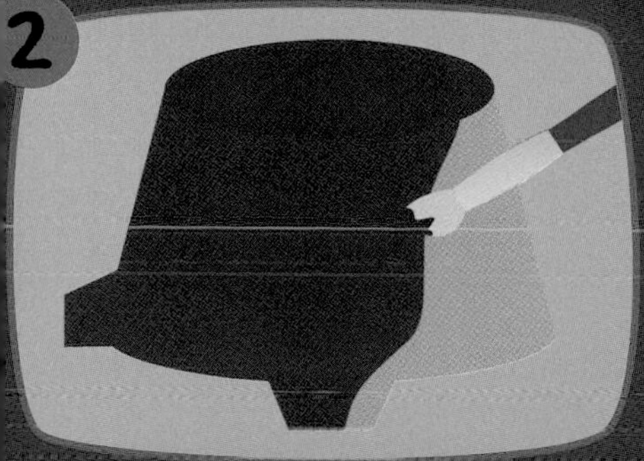

3 When dry, paint dark lines on the
eggbox to match Tiddles's shell.

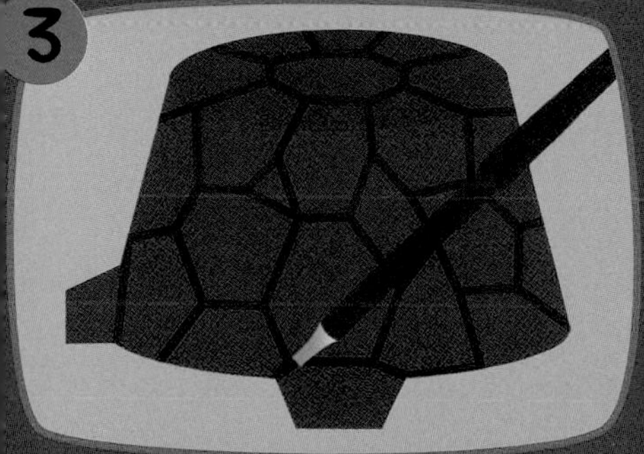

4 Glue the shell on to the body.
Then stick on the eyes and give
Tiddles a smiling red mouth.

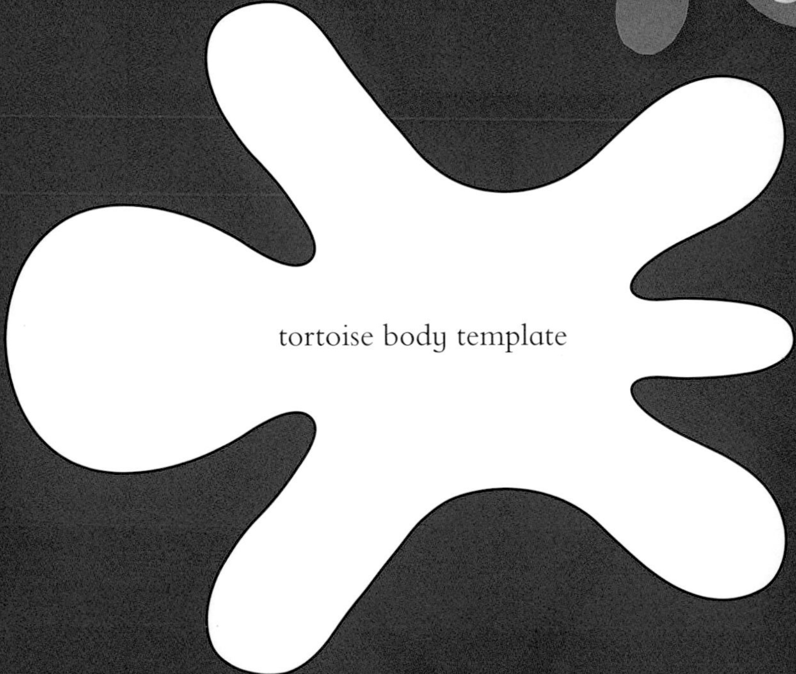

tortoise body template

Jigsaw Birthday Card

Peppa is making a jigsaw birthday card for Suzy Sheep's birthday!

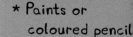

You will need
* Cardboard
* Paints or coloured pencil
* Paintbrush
* Black felt-tip p
* Ruler
* Pencil
* Scissors
* Envelope

1 Cut the cardboard into a square measuring 15cm x 15cm.

2 Draw or paint a colourful picture on one side of the cardboard.

3 Draw the outline of a flower, heart or star in thick black felt-tip pen on the other side of the card. Write your birthday message inside the black outline.

4 Using a ruler and pencil, divide the cardboard into 9 squares, each measuring 5cm x 5cm, then cut along the lines.

Your friend will have to do the jigsaw to read your Happy Birthday message!

Post the jigsaw pieces in an envelope.

Happy Birthday!
Love from
Peppa
X

89 Birdie Birthday Card

This birthday card has a surprise inside – a birdie with a pop-up beak!

You will need:
* Orange, yellow and pink card
* Scissors
* PVA glue
* Googly eyes
* Feathers
* Felt-tip pens

1

Fold a piece of orange card in half and cut a slit across the fold, as shown.

2

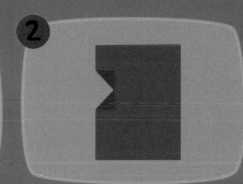

Fold back the flaps, then push the folded flaps inside your card to make the beak.

3

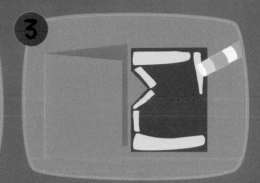

Glue a pink piece of card (the same size as the orange piece) behind the orange card, taking care not to stick it to the beak.

4

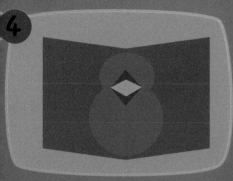

Cut out a curved shape from yellow card for the bird's head and body. Ask an adult to cut a diamond shape to fit the beak through. Stick inside the card.

Glue on some googly eyes and bright colourful feathers!

Don't glue the pink card behind the beak or the chick's mouth won't open!

Decorate the front of the card with the words "Happy Birthday!" or any design you like!

The flaps open like a beak when you open the card!

Dinosaur Prints

Here's how to make some roaringly good dinosaur wrapping paper and matching gift tags.

1 Use the templates to cut the dinosaur figure shape and the dinosaur footprint shape out of craft foam.

2 Glue the shapes on to corks or on to small blocks of wood or boxes to make them easier to print with.

3 Brush paint on to the foam shapes, then press down on to the paper to make each print.

4 Cut out some of your dinosaur prints and glue them on to pieces of cardboard to make gift tags.

footprint template

dinosaur template

Make a hole in the top of the gift tag with a hole punch and thread through some ribbon.

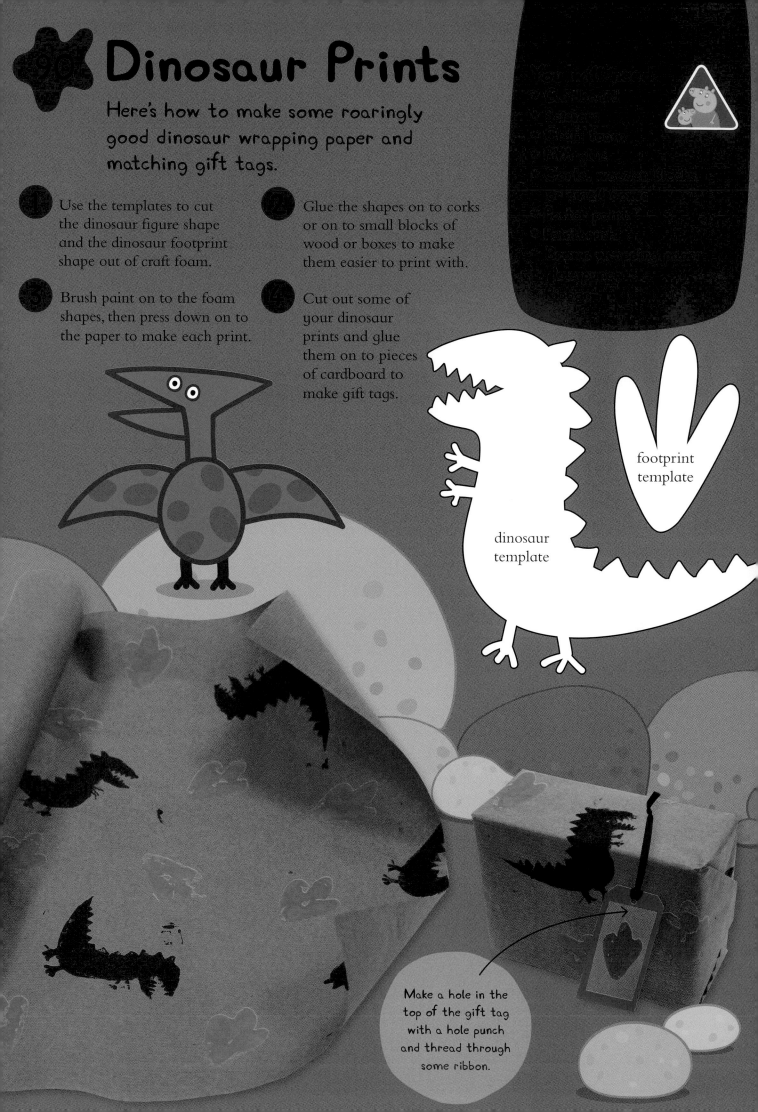

Paint George's Dinosaur

Would you like to paint a green dinosaur like George's?

You will need:
* Paper
* Green paint
* Paintbrush
* Googly eyes
* PVA glue

1 First paint a big C-shape on your paper, like this:

2 Paint two straight lines going in from the ends, for the dinosaur's wide-open mouth.

3 Paint a long curved line to make the dinosaur's back and tail.

4 Then draw a curved line for the dinosaur's tummy. Make sure the lines meet in a point, to make the dinosaur's tail.

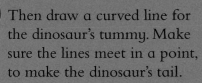

5 Paint two little arms . . .

6 . . . and legs.

7 Next, colour in your outline with green paint.

8 Add blobs of paint down the dinosaur's back to make it look spiky.

9 Last of all, glue on two googly eyes.

Grrr!

Paper-plate Dinosaur

This paper-plate dinosaur also looks like George's green dinosaur.

You will need:
* Paper plate
* Scissors
* Green paint
* Split pins
* Felt-tip pens

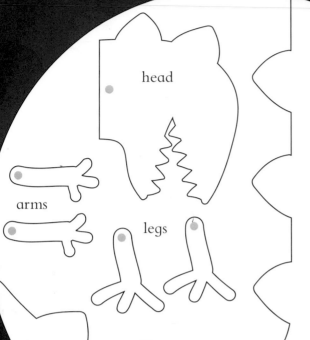

head

hole for head

arms

holes for arms

legs

body

holes for legs

1

2

3

Dine-saw!

93 Make Up a Dinosaur Story

Peppa and George have travelled back in time to the land of the dinosaurs. Everything is very quiet when suddenly some dinosaurs appear! ROOOOAAR! Make up a story about what happens next . . .

94 Move Like a Dinosaur

Some dinosaurs stood on two legs, some walked on four, some flew and some swam. Pretend to be a dinosaur and stomp and roar!

Puffy Paints

Make some puffy paints, then use them to paint a puffy-paint picture!

1 Mix together the flour, water and salt with a few drops of food colouring. Put the mixture into a squeezy bottle.

2 Make up lots of bottles of puffy paint – use a different one for each colour!

Puffy-paint Picture Frame

Here's how to make a picture frame decorated with your home-made puffy paint.

You will need:
* Thick cardboard
* Scissors
* Ruler
* Pencil
* PVA glue
* Coloured paint
* Paintbrush
* Puffy paints

1 Cut out two pieces of thick cardboard, the size you want your picture frame to be.

2 Cut a window in one piece of cardboard.

3 Glue the front of the frame to the back, leaving one side open so you can slide in a photograph.

4 Paint the front and back of the frame with thick coloured paint.

When dry, squeeze puffy paint shapes and squiggles on to your frame.

Once the puffy-paint decorations are dry, slide your photograph into the frame.

97 Eggbox Train

Toot! Toot! This little eggbox train looks like Grandpa Pig's *Gertrude*.

You will need:

* Two cardboard tubes
* Scissors
* Masking tape
* Pipe cleaners
* Old newspaper
* PVA glue
* Water
* White card
* Coloured card
* Cardboard eggbo[x]
* Acrylic paints
* Paintbrush
* Tissue paper
* Bottle top
* 1p coin
* Pencil
* Darning needle

1 Cut one tube in half and tape it to the top of the other tube to make the large funnel.

2 Scrunch up tissue paper to make the smaller funnel and tape in place.

3 Draw around the end of the engine tube on some card, cut out and tape it to the front end of the engine tube.

4 Copy the shape shown for the back of the engine on to card, cut it out and secure it to the back of the engine tube with tape.

5 Cover the engine in papier mâché and leave to dry.

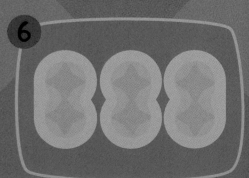

6 To make the carriages, cut the lid off the eggbox and then carefully cut the base of the eggbox into three pieces. Trim the longer edges so they're level with the other sides.

7

Once the papier mâché on the engine has dried, paint it white and leave it to dry.

8

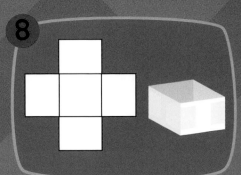

Copy the shape shown above on to card to make the driver's carriage. Fold and tape the sides together to make a box.

9

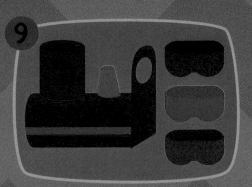

Paint the engine, driver's carriage and eggbox carriages to look like *Gertrude* and leave to dry.

10

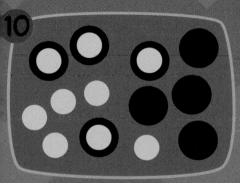

Draw around a bottle top on black card and cut out lots of wheels. Draw around a 1p coin on grey card, cut the circles out and stick them in the middle of the black circles to make the wheels' centres.

11

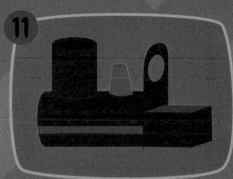

Glue the driver's carriage on to the back of the engine.

12

Make holes with a darning needle and thread the pipe cleaners through to join the carriages together. Glue on the wheels to finish.

See Make 5 for how to make papier mâché.

98 Little Brown Owl

Suzy Sheep loves her toy owl! Here's how to make a little toy owl.

You will need
* Felt, craft foam or card
* Scissors
* Black buttons
* PVA glue
* Ribbon
* Sticky tape

1 Copy or trace the templates on to card, then use them to cut pieces out of foam, felt or coloured card.

2 Glue the pieces together as shown below, then tape a loop of ribbon behind the owl's head so you can hang it up.

Stick on two black buttons to complete the owl's eyes.

templates

Talent Show

Peppa is very good at dancing, drawing and acting in plays!

Put on a talent show for your family and friends.

Your talent could be playing a musical instrument . . .

telling a joke . . .

reading a poem . . .

singing a song . . .

or doing a cartwheel!

showing everyone a picture you have drawn . . .

What's your talent?

100 Do a Ribbon Dance

Hold the ends of two pieces of wide, silky ribbon. What patterns can you make with the ribbon as you dance?

Shadow Animals

Peppa and her friends are having fun making shadow animals on the wall. Here are some shadow animals for you to try.

Shine a light on to a white wall. Make shadows by holding your hands between the light and the wall.

Open and close your hands to make your bird fly!

Bird
Cross your hands with your palms facing you and lock your thumbs together.

Swan
Bend one arm at the elbow and close your hand to make the head. Make the wing with your other hand.

Snail
Make one hand into a fist and rest it on the back of the other, outstretched hand.

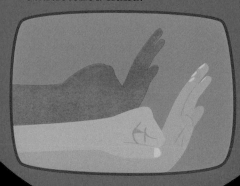

Spider
Cross your hands with your palms facing yourself. Lock your thumbs and tuck them down to make the spider's head, then wriggle your fingers so they look like the spider's legs.

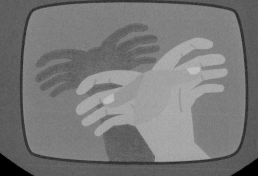

02 Shadow Puppets

If you like making shadow animals, put on a play using these shadow puppets!

templates

Make up a story as you move your shadow puppets around!

Trace or copy the templates on to cardboard and cut out. Then glue them on to craft sticks or long wooden chopsticks. Shine a lamp on to a wall and hold up the puppets so they cast a shadow.

Goldie Goldfish

Make this picture to show Peppa's pet goldfish, Goldie, swimming in her fish bowl!

You will need:
* Blue paper
* Paint
* Your fingers!
* Felt-tip pen

1 Print Goldie's body with a thumb dipped into orange paint. Print the tail with the tip of a finger.

2 When the paint is dry, draw on two eyes and a mouth.

3 Add some bubbles with your little finger dipped in white paint.

Don't forget to give Goldie a smiley mouth!

Paper Hat

All you need to make this paper hat is a big sheet of newspaper!

1

Fold the sheet of newspaper in half, then turn it round so the folded edge is at the top.

2

Fold down both of the top corners to the centre, so they meet in the middle.

3

Turn up about 10cm of the bottom of one side of the newspaper, over the triangles.

4

Flip over the paper and turn up the bottom edge on the other side, to match.

5

Fold over the outside edges at each side and tape them together.

6

Open out your hat and it's ready to wear!

Little Sprout's Vegetable Prints

It's fun to print with vegetables, says Little Sprout! Here are some vegetables you can try printing with.

You will need:
* Poster paints
* Saucers
* Cut-up vegetables (see list for ideas)
* Large sheets of paper

1 Ask an adult to cut up an assortment of vegetables and set out saucers containing different colours of paint.

2 Make patterns or print a picture using lots of different vegetables, by dipping the vegetables in the paint and pressing them down on the paper.

Vegetables to try:
• Half a sprout
• Half an apple
• Slices of carrot
• Slices of mushroom
• Half a potato

See Make 23 for how to cut printing blocks out of potatoes!

Cress Heads

Grow some green cress hair in these eggshell heads.

You will need:
* Eggshells
* Felt-tip pens
* Googly eyes
* Potting compost or cotton wool
* Cress seeds
* Water

1

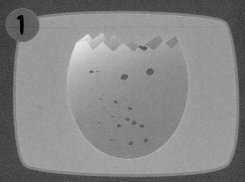

Save the shell after you've eaten a boiled egg, and then carefully clean and dry it.

2

Draw a funny face on the egg with felt-tip pens, or glue on some googly eyes.

3

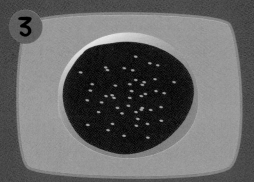

Fill the shell with potting compost or cotton wool. Add water and sprinkle on some cress seeds.

4

Put your egghead in a sunny spot and wait for its green cress hair to grow!

Use your cress to make some tasty egg-and-cress sandwiches!

Stand in an eggbox to keep them steady.

Plant Some Herbs

Plant a herb garden in a big flower pot.

1 Sow the seeds into the potting compost, following the instructions on the packets.

2 Put the pot or pots on to a window ledge.

3 Write the names of the herbs you have planted on to lolly sticks and put them in the soil.

4 Remember to water your herbs as they grow!

Some herbs to try:
- mint
- parsley
- chives
- thyme
- oregano
- basil

---

108 # Minty Dip

Here's how to make a delicious dip using your own home-grown mint!

You will need:
- * Large tub thick Greek yoghurt
- * Handful fresh mint
- * Quarter cucumber
- * Knife
- * Bowl
- * Cheese grater
- * Salt and pepper, to taste

1 Ask an adult to slice the cucumber in half lengthways and remove the seeds with a teaspoon.

2 Ask an adult to grate the cucumber and finely chop the mint into a bowl.

3 Mix in the yoghurt with a little salt and pepper.

Serve your minty dip with sticks of crunchy carrots, cucumber and celery!

If you like the taste, you can add a clove of crushed garlic, too.

Splitter! Splatter!

Make a splatter painting by flicking paint on to a big sheet of paper with a brush.

You will need
* Paper
* Poster paints
* Paintbrushes
* Water
* Scissors
* Glue

1 Lay out a large sheet of paper or unroll some lining paper.

2 Water down some poster paints, then flick the paint on to the paper with a brush.

Sea background made from splattering lots of different shades of blue paint.

Mummy Pig says this is a good activity to do outside!

Once dry, cut into wavy strips and stick on to some white paper.

Orange splatter-painting fish.

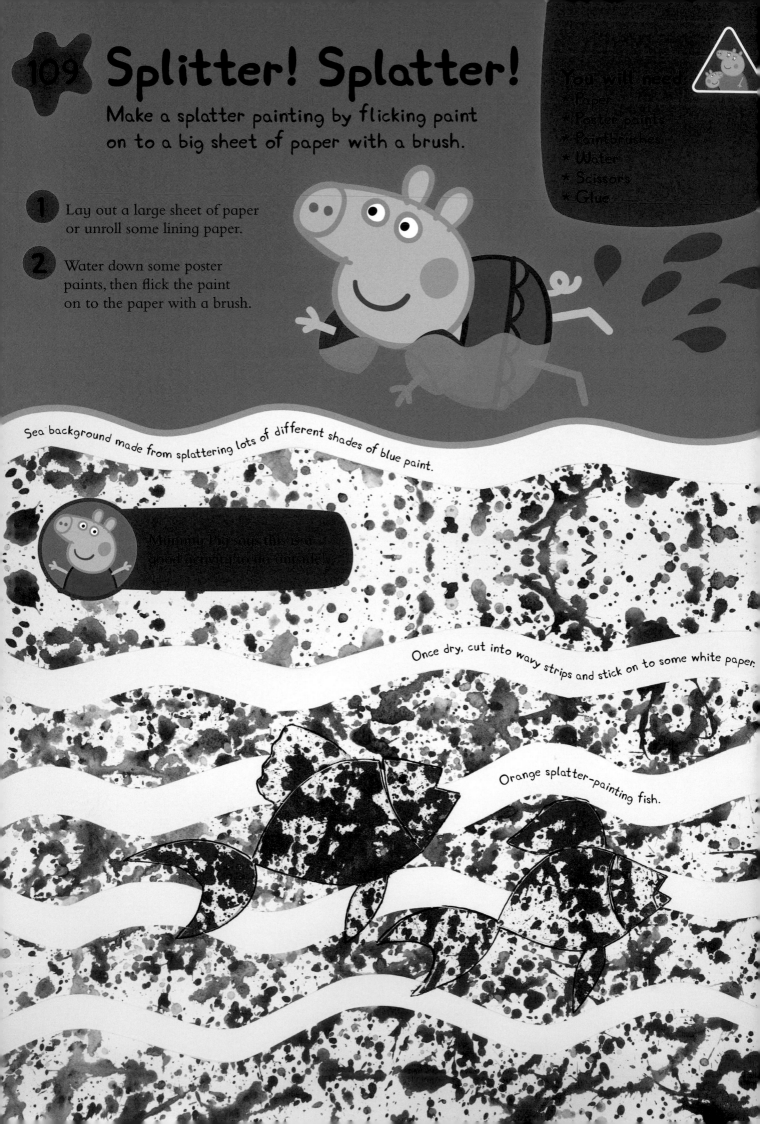

110 Rocket Lift-off

10, 9, 8, 7, 6, 5, 4, 3, 2, 1 . . . Blast off!
Make this rocket and watch it zoom
into space!

You will need:
* Paper
* Scissors
* Coloured paints, pens or pencils
* Drinking straw
* PVA glue

1 Use the template to draw
and cut out two identical
rocket shapes.

2 Glue the sides and the top
of the rocket together,
but not the bottom.

3 Colour your rocket with
poster paints, felt-tip pens
or coloured pencils.

4 Push the end of a straw into
the bottom of the rocket.

Blow through the straw to
make your rocket lift off!

template

Space Mobile

Use the templates to make this space mobile to hang in your bedroom.

You will need:
* Cardboard
* Scissors
* Paints
* Paintbrush
* Ribbon or string
* Hole punch
* Wooden chopsticks

1

Wrap ribbon or string around the centre of two wooden chopsticks to tie them together at right angles.

2

Copy or trace the templates on to cardboard. Cut out the shapes, then paint or colour in both sides.

3

Use a hole punch to make holes in the tops of the shapes. Attach the shapes to the chopsticks with ribbon or string, then hang the mobile from the ceiling.

moon template

star template

planet template

rocket template

112 Make Up a Space Story

Blast off! One day, two daring astronauts took off into space in their rocket and landed on the moon. They stepped out of their rocket and discovered . . .

Make up a space story about what the brave astronauts found on the moon.

Space Picture

Make this colourful picture of a rocket whizzing through space, past the stars and planets.

You will need:
* Paper
* Wax crayons
* Black watercolour paint
* Paintbrush

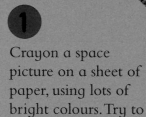

1

Crayon a space picture on a sheet of paper, using lots of bright colours. Try to fill the whole page.

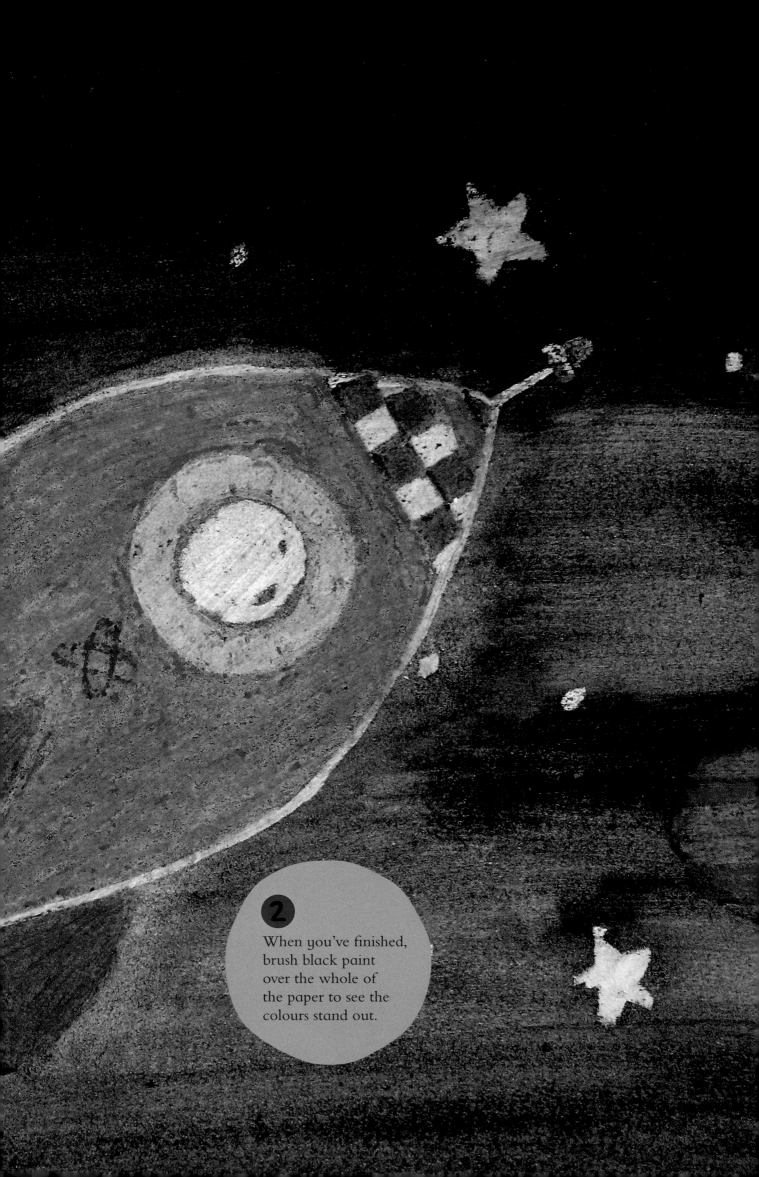

2

When you've finished, brush black paint over the whole of the paper to see the colours stand out.

Pizza Faces

Peppa and her friends are having a pizza party! Here's how to make some funny pizza faces.

You will need:
* Pizza bases
* Tomato sauce
* Toppings (see box for ideas)

1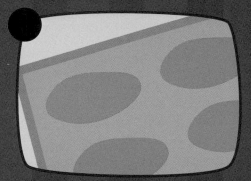

Make and roll out pizza dough, or use ready-made pizza bases.

2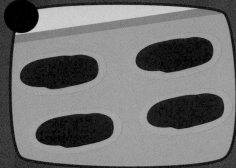

Spread a thin layer of tomato sauce on to each base.

3

Add your favourite toppings to make a funny face, or a pattern.

4 Ask a grown-up to bake each pizza in a preheated oven at 180°C fan/200°C (gas mark 6) for 8–10 minutes.

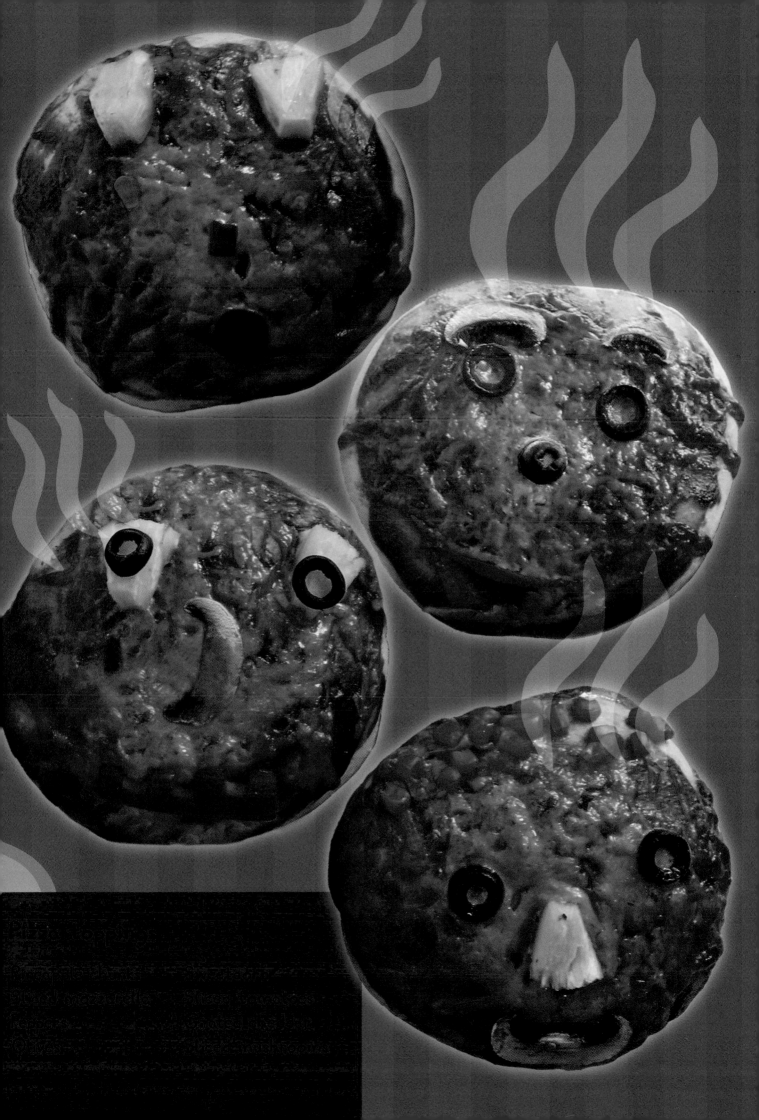

Halloween Lanterns

Make a scary pumpkin lantern to frighten your friends at Halloween!

1

Ask an adult to cut the top off a large pumpkin.

2

Scoop out the soft insides and seeds with a spoon.

3

Draw a spooky Halloween face on the front.

4

Ask an adult to cut out the eyes, nose and mouth.

5

Put a nightlight inside, ready for Halloween.

You can carve a watermelon if you don't have a pumpkin.

Ask an adult to light the candle when it gets dark.

Peppa and George have been invited to
a Halloween party with all their friends.
"Let's tell spooky stories," says Peppa.
"You start, Peppa," says Suzy Sheep.
"Once upon a time, a wicked witch turned
a little pig into a frog . . ." says Peppa.
George looks worried.
What happens next?

Spooky Bats

Hang up a chain of spooky black bats at Halloween!

1.

2.

3.

4.

5.

template

Make more bats and glue them together into one really long chain!

See Make 71 for how to make a concertina.

Witch's Cloak

Dress up as a witch this Halloween.
Here's how to make a black witch's cloak.

You will need:
* Black fabric
* Silver fabric or card covered in silver foil
* Pinking shears
* Black ribbon or tape
* Fabric glue
* Measuring tape
* Pegs or large paperclips

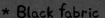

Taking measurements
Measure how long you want the cloak to be, from the back of the neck to the hem.

Next, measure from the neck to the wrist.

Double both measurements to cut out the right-sized piece of fabric for the cloak.

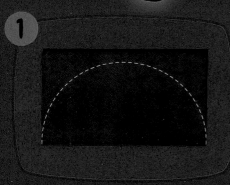

1 Fold the fabric in half, then cut out a large semicircle, using pinking shears so the fabric does not fray.

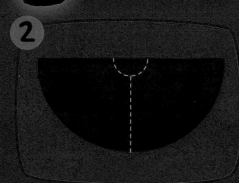

2 Cut a shallow neckline and a slit down the centre of the top layer of fabric.

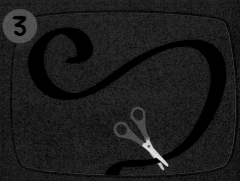

3 Cut a piece of black ribbon, long enough to go round the neck, plus an extra 40cm.

4 Drizzle fabric glue along the inside edge of the neck, fold the fabric down over the ribbon and glue, leaving 20cm free at each side.

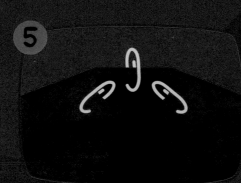

5 Hold the fabric and ribbon together with large paperclips or pegs while the glue dries.

6 Cut stars and a moon out of silver fabric and glue them on to the cloak, or glue on card shapes covered in silver foil.

Witch's Hat

Don't forget to make a witch's hat like Candy Cat's!

You will need:
* Scissors
* Compass
* PVA glue
* Black sugar paper and thin black card
* Silver foil
* Ruler
* Pencil

1 Draw a semicircle on a large sheet of black sugar paper with the straight edge measuring 30cm. Cut out the shape, roll the paper into a cone and glue.

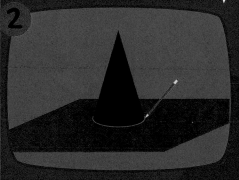

2 Draw around the bottom of the cone on to a piece of black card.

3 Draw a circle 1.5cm bigger and another 3cm smaller.

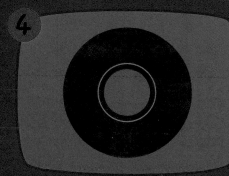

4 Cut out the large circle, then cut out the small circle, as shown.

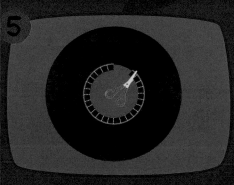

5 Cut lines from the inside of the circle to the pencil line, then fold up the tabs.

6 Dab glue on to the tabs and attach the brim to the bottom of the cone.

7 Stick silver foil stars on the hat.

120 Meringue Ghosts

These crunchy ghost meringues are perfect for a Halloween party.

You will need:
* 2 eggs
* Pinch of salt
* 100g caster sugar
* Currants or glacé cherries
* Baking paper

To separate the egg whites:

Crack an egg in half and pour the yolk from one half of the shell to the other, letting the white fall into a bowl.

1 Beat the whites of the eggs and a pinch of salt in a bowl with a whisk until the mixture forms soft peaks.

2 Whisk the caster sugar into the egg whites a little at a time until the meringue looks glossy white.

3 Lay a sheet of baking paper over a baking tray. Spread tablespoonfuls of mixture on to the baking paper.

4 Bake the ghosts for 4–5 hours in an oven at its lowest setting until the meringue mixture is firm. Allow to cool on the tray before enjoying.

Shape the mixture into ghost shapes with the back of a teaspoon.

Give your ghosts tiny currant eyes and, if you like, sliced cherry mouths.

Putting the oven on its lowest setting keeps the meringues white, like ghosts!

121 Spooky Spider

This black wool pom-pom spider is perfect for Halloween!

You will need:
* Cardboard
* Scissors
* Black wool
* Black elastic
* Googly eyes
* Black pipe cleaners
* PVA glue

Make a black wool pom-pom (see Make 47). Here, instead of tying wool between the card circles, use a long piece of elastic so the spider can bounce up and down.

Cut out a semicircle in blue card for a smiley mouth.

Glue on two googly eyes and 8 bendy black pipe-cleaner legs.

Hang your pom-pom spider in the corner of a room to make someone jump!

122 Sock Puppet

This stripy red dragon puppet is made from an old sock!

You will need:
* Old sock
* Scissors
* Felt or craft foam
* Fabric glue
* Googly eyes
* Coloured felt-tip pens
* Pipe cleaner
* Heavy-duty tape

1
Cut two circles from coloured felt or craft foam, slightly larger than your googly eyes. Glue the eyes to these circles and then glue them to the front side of the sock, almost opposite the heel.

2
Cut 7 small triangles from white felt or craft foam. Glue three to the bottom of the mouth opening and four to the top of the mouth opening to make the teeth.

3
Cut two large triangles from coloured felt or craft foam, and glue them along the top edge of the sock, behind the eyes.

4
Cut out two wing shapes from coloured felt or craft foam. Using a dark pen, draw on the wing spines to define the shape. Glue one wing either side of the sock about halfway down the sock length.

5
Twist the end of a pipe cleaner to create the forked tongue, then poke the opposite end through the mouth opening between the toes and the heel.

6
Adjust the pipe cleaner to the desired length and trim the end, making sure no sharp wire sticks out. Then attach inside the sock using either glue or heavy-duty tape.

When gluing on all the components, it helps to put the sock on your hand to get everything in the right position.

123 Paper-plate Fish

These funky fish have been made out of paper plates!

You will need:
* Paper plates
* Scissors
* PVA glue
* Paint
* Paintbrush
* Tissue paper
* White, black and coloured card

Cut a triangle out of the paper plate to make the fish's open mouth.

Glue the triangle on to the back of the plate to make the fish's tail.

Paint your fish
bright colours.

To make the fish
scales, fold a sheet
of tissue paper in half
several times. Cut out
an oval shape, separate
the pieces and glue
on to the body.

Cut out circles
of coloured, white
and black card and
stick one on top of
the other for the
fish's eye.

124 Daddy Pig's Orange Cheesecake

Daddy Pig and George are making a no-bake cheesecake, decorated with tasty little pieces of orange.

1 Put all the biscuits into a plastic freezer bag and crush them with a rolling pin until they look like fine breadcrumbs. Pour them in a large bowl.

2 Prepare the gelatine using the instructions on the packet, then set to one side. Whisk the cream in a separate bowl until it forms soft peaks.

3 Add the melted butter to the crushed biscuits and mix together. Pour the mixture into the tin, press down firmly, then put it in the fridge.

4 Mix the melted chocolate, cream cheese and orange zest in another bowl until smooth. Add 3 tbsp of prepared gelatine, mix well, then fold in the whipped cream.

5 Remove the tin from the fridge. Pour the filling on top of the biscuit base, then put the tin back in the fridge for an hour, until the topping sets.

6 After an hour, make 300ml of orange jelly using the instructions on the packet. Leave the jelly to cool, then pour it on top of the cheesecake. Put the cheesecake back in the fridge until the jelly has set.

You will need:
* 120g ginger nut biscuits, crushed
* 120g digestive biscuits, crushed
* 23cm loose-bottomed tin
* 100g butter, melted
* Plastic freezer bag
* Whisk
* Rolling pin
* Mixing bowls

To make the filling:
* 11g powdered gelatine
* 375ml double cream
* 250g white chocolate, melted
* 400g cream cheese
* zest of one orange
* 300ml orange jelly (made from cubes or powder)
* 1 tin orange segments

Carefully take the cheesecake out of the tin and decorate it with orange segments. Yum Yum! Snort!

For a vegetarian version, use a vegetarian gelatine substitute instead of powdered gelatine for the filling, and leave off the orange-jelly topping.

125 Feed the Birds

Make a feeding ball to feed the birds in the wintertime.

You will need: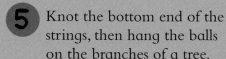
* Leftover dry kitchen scraps, such as oats, raisins, sultanas, bread, cake, peanuts or grated cheese
* Lard or suet (around half the amount of the dry mixture)
* Saucepan
* Wooden spoon
* String

1 Mix your dry ingredients in a bowl.

2 Melt some lard or suet in a saucepan, pour it over the dry mixture and stir it together.

3 When the mixture has cooled, shape it into balls around long pieces of string.

4 Put the balls in the fridge to set for several hours or leave them overnight.

5 Knot the bottom end of the strings, then hang the balls on the branches of a tree.

Falling Snowflakes

These pretty decorations
are easy to make.

You will need:
* Square sheets of
  white paper
* Scissors
* Pencil
* White thread
* Sticky tape

1 Fold a sheet of paper in
half, then in half again
to make a smaller square.

2 On the open side, cut a curve
from one corner to the other so
that, if you opened the paper out,
you would have a rough circle.

3 Keeping the paper folded, draw
some random shapes on one side,
then cut them out.

4 Unfold the paper to reveal your
pretty snowflake.

5 Tape a piece of white thread to
the top of your snowflake and
hang them around the room or
on your Christmas tree.

127 Snowy Scene

Make a magic snowy-scene picture!

You will need:
* Paper
* White crayon or candle
* Blue paint
* Paintbrush
* Coloured pencils

It's MAGIC!

Use coloured pencils to draw the trees and details such as the aerial, windows and door.

1 Use a white crayon or a white candle and draw a picture of a snowy day on a sheet of white paper. Make sure you draw lots of big white snowflakes!

2 When you've finished, paint the paper with some watery blue paint and see your picture appear.

128 Build a Snowman

Look! It's snowing! Peppa and George have built a snowman. Next time it snows where you live, why not build a snowman, too?

1 Roll a big ball of snow for the snowman's body.

2 Roll a smaller ball for the snowman's head and put it on top.

3 Use two pebbles or lumps of charcoal for the snowman's eyes, a carrot for his nose and some twigs for his arms.

4 Wrap a woolly scarf around your snowman's neck and pop a woolly hat on his head!

129 Snowman Faces

Make some fun paper-plate snowman faces to put on your wall.

You will need:
* Scissors
* Paper plate
* White tissue paper or cotton-wool balls
* PVA glue
* Orange felt or card
* Black buttons
* Black and coloured card or sugar paper

Don't forget to give your snowman a hat and scarf!

Hat cut from green cardboard or sugar paper

Green card scarf

1 Glue balls of cotton wool or scrunched-up balls of white tissue paper all over your paper plate.

2 Glue on a piece of orange card or felt, cut into a triangle, for the snowman's nose.

3 Add two black button eyes and a mouth of glued-on buttons or card circles.

130 Granny Pig's Apple and Blackberry Crumble

This tasty crumble is perfect on a cold winter's day!

You will need
for the crumble:
* 300g plain flour
* 175g sugar
* 200g butter, cubed

For the filling:
* 300g apples
* 150g blackberries
* 50g sugar

1 Rub the butter into the flour with your fingertips, so the mixture looks like fine breadcrumbs, then stir in the sugar.

2 Peel the apples, remove the cores, then cut into 1cm–2cm pieces. Wash the blackberries, then pat dry.

3 Put the fruit into a greased ovenproof dish, around 24cm wide. Sprinkle the sugar over the fruit, then pour the crumble mixture over the top.

4 Bake the crumble in a preheated oven at 180°C for around 40–45 minutes until the top is golden brown.

Granny Pig says . . .

If you like, add a sprinkle of cinnamon over the fruit mixture before you add the crumble mix.

Serve your apple and blackberry crumble with ice cream, thick cream or custard. Yum!

131 Penguin Pals

These cute little penguins are made from cardboard tubes.

You will need:
* Cardboard tubes
* Black poster paint or acrylic paint
* Paintbrush
* Googly eyes
* White paper
* Orange card
* PVA glue
* Scissors

1 Paint some cardboard tubes with black paint.

2 When the paint is dry, glue on a white paper chest and a pair of googly eyes.

penguin wings and feet template

Wings cut from black card.

Stick on two orange card feet and an orange beak!

Mini Christmas Tree

Make this mini Christmas tree from a cone of cardboard. Don't forget to put the star on top!

1 Draw round a plate on to green card, then cut a line to the centre.

2 Twist the card into a cone-shape and stick the edges together.

3 Glue some ribbon round the tree, then add some stick-on gems.

4 Copy the star template on to card, cover it in foil, then glue it on top.

star template

133 Christmas Tree Decorations

Use cookie cutters to make these decorations to hang on your Christmas tree!

See Make 24 for instructions on how to make salt dough.

You can also make these decorations using self-hardening modelling clay.

gold glitter tinsel

swirls of silver glitter

stick-on gems

You will need:
* Salt dough
* Rolling pin
* Cookie cutters (star, tree, circle)
* Skewer or toothpick
* Poster paints
* PVA glue
* Water
* Ribbon or wool
* Glitter
* Stick-on gems

1 Roll out some salt dough with a rolling pin until around 0.5cm thick.

2 Cut trees, stars and circles out of the dough with cookie cutters.

3 Make holes in the top of each decoration with a skewer or toothpick.

4 Bake until hard, and leave to cool. Paint, leave to dry, then varnish and decorate.

5 Loop wool or ribbon through the holes to hang them on your tree.

See Make 46 for how to varnish.

Snowman

Make a little snowman out of clay, small enough to fit in a glittery snow globe!

You will need:
* Oven-hardening modelling clay – green, orange, black and white
* Water
* Cocktail sticks

1

Roll out two balls of white clay, making one slightly smaller than the other.

2

Join the balls with a little water. Using the coloured clay, give your snowman a hat, scarf, eyes, mouth and a carrot nose.

3

Make two gloves and place them on the ends of cocktail sticks. Push the sticks into the sides of the snowman's body. Bake the snowman in the oven according to the instructions on the packet.

Snow Globe

Pop your clay snowman into a globe made from a plastic jar and shake it to make it snow!

You will need:
* Plastic jar with screw-on lid
* Very strong glue
* Clay snowman or a small toy
* Glitter
* Glycerin
* Water

1 Ask an adult to stick your snowman on to the inside of the jar's lid using very strong glue. Thicken some water with some glycerin, pour the mixture in the jar, then add some glitter.

2 Screw on the lid and give your globe a shake!

Felt Christmas Stocking

Make this little felt Christmas stocking to hang on your Christmas tree!

1

Copy or trace the template on to card and cut out two stocking shapes in red felt.

2

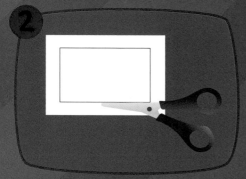

Cut out a rectangle of white felt, to fit the top of the stocking.

3

Glue the felt pieces together with fabric glue. Glue the strip of white felt across the top.

4

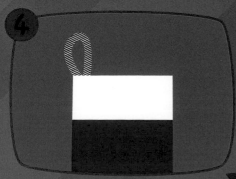

Cut some ribbon and glue inside the top of the stocking to make a hanging loop.

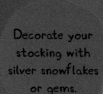

Decorate your stocking with silver snowflakes or gems.

Add some green felt in the shape of a triangle to look just like a Christmas tree!

felt Christmas stocking template

Make Up a Christmas Story

It's Christmas Eve and the house is quiet and still. What's that noise?

Peppa tiptoes downstairs and there, in the living room, is Santa . . . and he's fast asleep!

"Wake up, Santa," cries Peppa. "You still have lots of presents to deliver!"
"Oh dear!" says Santa. "Please will you help me, Peppa?"
Make up a story about Peppa helping Santa deliver presents to her friends.

138 Action-hero Cape

Look...
hero...
cloak...

You will need:
* Old, adult-sized T-shirt
* Scissors
* Felt or scrap of fabric
* PVA glue

1

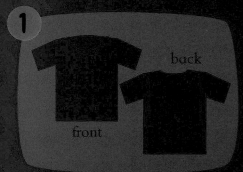

front   back

Cut down the centre...
around the armholes...
leaving the neck...

2 Cut a hero symbol...
and glue it on to the back...
of the T-shirt...
Peppa's action-hero symbol...
or make up your own!

Action-hero Wristbands

Make some matching wristbands to go with your cloak.

You will need:
- Cardboard tubes
- Scissors
- Paints
- Paintbrush
- Silver card
- PVA glue

1 Cut the cardboard tubes to make two lengths, each 4cm-5cm long. Cut down the sides of the tubes so they open out slightly.

2 Paint the tubes to match your cape. When the paint is dry, paint or glue on a matching action-hero symbol and some shiny silver bands.

140 Action-hero Mask

Now make an action-hero mask!

You will need:
* Black card
* Scissors
* Darning needle
* Black elastic

1 Copy or trace the template below on to black card and cut it out.

template

2 Cut out the eyeholes and make small holes in the sides of the mask with a darning needle.

3 Thread black elastic through the holes, measure to fit, then knot the elastic at each side.

Make Up an Action-hero Story

It is a quiet day at Madame Gazelle's playgroup and everyone is busy painting.

"Help! Help!" someone shouts from outside the window.
Oh no, it's Doctor Hamster. Her pet, Tiddles the tortoise, is stuck up a tree!

Don't panic! It's Pedro the action hero to the rescue! Make up a story about how Pedro saves the day!

Princess Peppa Book Cover

Cover one of your favourite books or notebooks, so it looks just like Peppa's princess book!

You will need:
* Sheets of dark pink and gold wrapping paper
* Scissors
* PVA glue
* Coloured pom-poms or stick-on gems
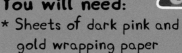

1

Open the book, lay it on the inside of a sheet of pink wrapping paper, then cut the paper so it is 4cm–5cm bigger than the book.

2

Cut diagonal lines from the edge of the paper to the centre of the book. Throw away the triangles of paper in the middle.

3

Fold over one side of the paper to fit the front cover of the book, then do the same at the back.

4

Fold down a triangle of paper in each corner, then fold over the edges and glue in place.

Use this template to cut out a gold Peppa crown to glue on to the book's new cover!

template

Decorate the crown with stick-on gems or coloured pom-poms.

Now you have a princess book that looks just like Peppa's!

All About Me Book

Start a scrapbook all about YOU!

Buy a blank notebook, or make one from folded sheets of coloured sugar paper. Glue in photos of yourself, your family and friends, tickets to places you've visited, wrappers of your favourite sweets, pictures of your favourite animals and some of your drawings.

You will need:
* A3 sheets of coloured sugar paper
* Pencil
* Darning needle
* Wool or thick string

To make a scrapbook:

1

Fold 5–6 sheets of A3 sugar paper in half.

2

Make a mark in the centre of the spine. Then make two marks above and below this mark.

3

Push a needle through all the marks to make holes.

4

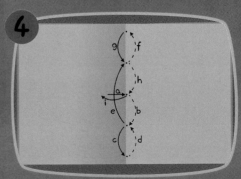

Thread a darning needle with wool or thick string. Push the needle through the centre hole, from the inside out, then sew in and out of the holes, following the letters on the drawing, ending with the wool coming out of the middle hole. Tie the ends of the wool together in a knot.

Sunflower Height Chart

Measure how tall you are growing on a giant sunflower height chart!

You will need:
* Long sheet of paper, such as wallpaper lining paper
* Paints
* Paintbrush
* Green card or paper
* Scissors
* Reusable adhesive putty

1 Paint a big sunflower with a long green stem on a sheet of lining paper and fix it to the wall.

2 Cut out some big green sunflower leaves.

3 Measure everyone's height against the sunflower stem and make a mark on the paper.

4 Write each person's name on a leaf and stick it on to the sunflower stem to show how tall they are.

5 Measure everyone's height again in a few months' time to see how much they have grown!

Handprint Trees

Use your hands to print some colourful trees!

Paint your hand with brown paint and press it on to a sheet of paper to make the tree's trunk and branches.

Dab on blobs of paint with a big brush or your fingertips to give your tree pink blossom, green leaves or orange and gold autumn colours.

146 Handprint Animals

You can also use your hands to make animal pictures.

Use different colours of paint to give your fish stripes.

Paint the head and neck in the same colour as your handprint. Then paint some orange legs and a beak.

Give your animals eyes and a smiley mouth with a black felt-tip pen.

147 Kazoo Comb

It's fun to make your own musical instruments like this kazoo comb.

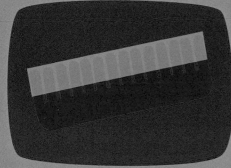

Fold a sheet of tissue paper over a large wide-toothed comb. Press your lips against the tissue-paper comb and hum!

148 Water Music

Fill glasses or jam jars with different amounts of water. Tap the glasses with a pencil or a metal spoon and listen to the different sounds!

If you like, add a few drops of food colouring to each glass to make the water different colours.

Chocolate Puddle Biscuits

Shape these tasty boot biscuits out of cookie dough and dip them in chocolate puddles! Yum! Yum!

1 Preheat the oven to 180°C (gas mark 4) and lightly grease a flat baking tray.

2 Mix together the butter and sugar, mix in the egg yolks, then stir in the flour.

3 Add just enough milk to bring the mixture together into a soft dough.

4 Sprinkle some flour on to a work surface. Divide the ball of dough into three pieces, divide each ball in half, then in half again, to make 12 balls.

5 Roll out each ball into a sausage shape. Turn up the bottom of each sausage and press it flat to make a boot shape.

6 Bake the biscuit boots for 10–15 minutes, until golden brown. Sprinkle with caster sugar, then leave to cool.

You will need:
* 100g butter, softened
* 100g caster sugar plus extra for sprinkling
* 2 egg yolks
* 200g plain flour, sifted
* 1–2 tablespoons milk
* Large bar of milk chocolate

Makes 12 biscuit boots

Dip the boots in the cooled muddy chocolate puddle – and eat! Snort!

Melt a large bar of milk chocolate in a microwave or over a pan of simmering water, then pour the chocolate into a shallow bowl.

Peppa loves muddy puddles, especially when they're made of chocolate!

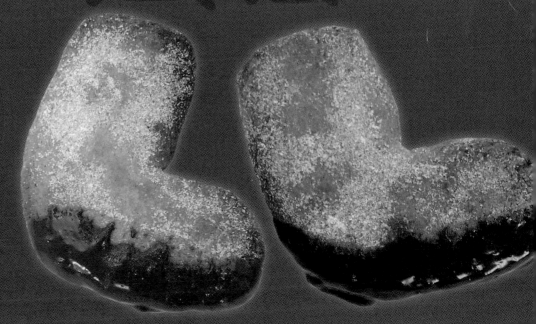

149 Maracas

These marvellous maracas are made from plastic bottles!

1. Make sure your plastic bottles are clean and dry, then pour in something that will make a noise when you shake it.

2. Screw on the bottle tops, put a cardboard tube over the top of each bottle and tape in place.

3. Cut lengths of masking tape or plastic duct tape, and wind around the tube to make a handle.

You will need:
* Clear plastic bottles
* Cardboard tubes
* Scissors
* Coloured masking tape or duct tape
* Paperclips, beads, dried peas or lentils
* Coloured ribbons

Fill each bottle around half full.

Get busy shaking!

Tie coloured ribbons round the top of the handle to decorate.